The Suit Case

Volume 7 of
The Casebooks
of Octavius Bear

Harry DeMaio

"Alternative Universe Mysteries for Adult
Animal Lovers"

Paperback ISBN 978-1-78705-291-8
ePub ISBN 978-1-78705-292-5
PDF ISBN 978-1-78705-293-2

Published in the UK by MX Publishing
335 Princess Park Manor, Royal Drive,
London, N11 3GX
www.mxpublishing.co.uk

Cover layout and construction by
Brian Belanger

Dedicated to GTP

A Most Extraordinary Bear

Acknowledgements

These books have evolved over a long period of time and under a wide range of influences and circumstances. I am indebted to many people for helping to bring Octavius and his cohorts to the printed page. Thanks most especially to my wife, Virginia, for her insights and clever suggestions as well as her unfailing enthusiasm for the project and patience with its author. To my sons, Mark and Andrew and their spouses, Cindy and Lorraine, for helping make these tomes more readable and audience friendly. To Cathy Hartnett, cheerleader-extraordinaire for her eagerness to see this alternate universe take form. To Jack Magan, Paul Bernish, Dan Andriacco, Amy Thomas, Luke Benjamin Kuhns and Zohreh Zand for their enthusiastic encouragement.

Kudos to Jim Effler, the late Bob Gibson and Brian Belanger for their wonderful illustrations and covers. Thanks, of course, to Steve Emecz and Timi at MX Publishing for giving Octavius et al. a great home

If, in spite of all this support, some errors or inconsistencies have crept through, the buck stops here. Needless to say, all the characters, situations, and narratives are fictional.

Also by Harry DeMaio

The Open and Shut Case

The Case of the Spotted Band

The Case of Scotch

The Lower Case

The Curse of the Mummy's Case

The Attaché Case

The Development of Civilization

Volume Seven - Part One

<u>Our Origins</u>

(From "An Introduction to Faunapology"
by Octavius Bear Ph.D.)

About 100,000 years ago, according to scientific experts, a colossal solar flare blasted out from our Sun, creating gigantic magnetic storms here on Earth. These highly charged electrical tempests caused startling physical and psychological imbalances in the then population of our world. The complete nervous systems of some species were totally destroyed. For example, "Homo Sapiens" lost all mental and motor capabilities and rapidly became extinct. Less developed species exposed to the radiation were affected differently. Four-footed and finned mammals, birds and reptiles suddenly found themselves capable of complex thought, enhanced emotions, self-awareness, social consciousness and the ability to communicate, sometimes orally, sometimes telepathically, often both. Both speech production and speech perception slowly progressed with the evolution of tongues, lips, vocal cords and enhanced ear to brain connections. Many species developed opposable digits, fingers or claws, further accelerating civilized progress. Some others (most fish and underground dwellers) were shielded from the radiation and remained only as sentient as they were before the blast. This event is referred to as 'The Big Shock'. It remains under intensive study.

The Players

- **Octavius Bear** – Mega-sized Kodiak; Narcoleptic war hero; Consulting Detective; Scientist; Inventor; Seeker of justice; Gazillionaire owner of Universal Ursine Industries; Gourmet/Gourmand; Bee Keeper; Somewhat sedentary and grouchy just on general principles.

- **Mauritius (Maury) Meerkat** – Narrator; Assistant to Octavius; Theatrical Agent; African *émigré* with a French-Dutch background; clever with a shady history.

- **Bearoness Belinda Béarnaise Bruin Bear** *(nee Black)* – Gorgeous polar superstar, with the Aquashow, *"Some Like It Cold."* Wife of Octavius; Extremely rich widow of Bearon Byron Bruin living in Polar Paradise in the Shetlands; Owner-pilot of the last flying Concorde SST

- **Arabella Bear** – Hybrid bear cub prodigy; Twin daughter of Bearoness Belinda and Octavius.

- **McTavish Bear** – Hybrid bear cub prodigy; Twin son of Bearoness Belinda and Octavius.

- **Mlle Woof** – Bichon Frisé – Governess to the twin cubs.

- **Frau Schuylkill** – Octavius' beautiful Swiss she-wolf estate manager/cook/pilot/security officer with many other mysterious and military talents. She rescued Octavius from his dive off the Breakurbach Falls while he was struggling with his nemesis, Imperius Drake.

- **Wyatt Where** – Another wolf; Former military intelligence officer who had retired to a security post at the Bank of Lake Michigan in Chicago and then quit to join Octavius.

- **Howard Watt** – Porcupine; High tech security authority who also left the Bank to join Octavius; Alternate Universe specialist; Laser and particle beam accelerator expert.

- **Otto the Magnificent – AKA Hairy Otter -** An absolutely terrible illusionist magician, Otto the Magnificent escaped the claws of super villain Imperius Drake but not before he developed some amazing powers courtesy of Imperius' genetic alterations.

- **Benedict and Galatea Tigris** – White Bengals – The Flying Tigers – Pilots of Belinda's and Octavius' aircraft – brother and sister.

- **Inspector Bruce Wallaroo** – Irrepressible but brilliant marsupial; an international law and order genius from Down Under; often calls on Octavius and Maury for support.

- **Chita** – Beautiful, fascinating, clever, sexy, immoral and highly independent feline who among other things, is the publisher and editor-in-chief of *PURR* and *SOW* magazines.

- **L. Condor** – Andean Condor; cyber-net genius with a twelve-foot wingspan and artificial voice.

- **Marlin** – Dolphin (sic) the Prince of Whales' Chief Scientist, Magician and part time Jester.

- **Wolford Wolverine Esq.** – Octavius' lawyer and UUI's chief counsel

- **Fetlock Holmes** – The Great Horse Detective and sometime associate of Octavius Bear

- **Professor Hercules Ovibos** – Muskox; self-styled inventive "genius"

- **Phileas Phox Esq.** – Weasel; Managing Partner of Phox, Fox and Foxx LLC law firm

- **Felicity Fox** – Ferret; Partner Phox, Fox and Foxx LLC law firm

- **Farrington Foxx** – Skunk; Partner Phox, Fox and Foxx LLC law firm
- **Detective Inspector Carlo Coyote** – Cincinnati Police Department
- **Detective Inspector Grizzly Ford** – Detroit Police Department
- **Special Agent Honey Badger** – Detroit FBI
- **Professor Karl Shepherd Ph.D.**- MIT Quantum Mechanics Laboratory
- **Doctor Susanna Shrike** – Director of Extraterrestrial Studies – Caltech
- **Commander Cornelius Cormorant** – US Navy Advanced Research Command
- **Alfred Armadillo** – Sr. VP Communication Technology – Goggle Plex
- **Covington Cougar**– Venture Capitalist with Space Enterprises LLC
- **General Turmoil** – Horse; Leader of The Business; Intent on Cosmic Conquest
- **The Protector** – Eagle on Home World (Biosphere X)
- **The Supreme Council** – Avian Raptor Leaders of Home World (Biosphere X)
- **Hawk and Falcon** - Home World Heavies
- **Ursula** – Universal Ursine Intellect Model 6 – Artificial Intelligence System

Locations

Cincinnati, Ohio; UUI, Kentucky; Detroit, Michigan; Polar Paradise in the Shetlands, Cape Canaveral, Florida and Alternate Universes

Octavius

Prologue

Do Bears give you a scare? Well, me too.
So, I'll pass on this tactic to you.
You just fix that old Bear
With a cold, piercing stare.
But make sure that he's Winnie-the-Pooh.

"All right Wolford! Stay on it and keep me posted!"

Slam!!

Octavius ripped off his oversized head set and threw it across the office. I wouldn't want to jump to conclusions but I suspect he is upset.

"What tidings of comfort and joy has our legal eagle brought us this time?"

"He's a Wolverine, as if you didn't know and he says our prize pain litigant is at it again. I don't know, Maury. I guess UUI *(Universal Ursine Industries)* is too big a target to escape frivolous lawsuits but this time Professor Hercules Ovibos has gone well beyond the limits. He's a greedy nut whose only inventions have been imaginary grounds for taking us to court. That Muskox is also an extortionist par excellence. This time he says we have willfully stolen his intellectual property for developing sub-atomic propulsion systems."

"What are sub-atomic propulsion systems?"

"Damned if I know. If we're working on anything that even sounds like that, I should be the first to know and I don't. Give me back my headset. I'm going to call UUI Power Division management and Howard Watt and get to the bottom of this. Maury, ask Ursula to enlighten us."

While I skitter across the room and retrieve the Great Bear's slightly battered communication device, let me take a moment and do a few introductions. Once he gets himself re-attached he'll be chewing up the network for quite a while.

First, a few words about myself. Mauritius Meerkat at your service. Just call me Maury. At slightly over two feet tall plus tail and weighing in at twenty-three pounds, I am Octavius' number one assistant, sidekick and verbal punching bag. I am a pretty clever detective in my own right and have a few sidelines such as theatrical agent for several very talented animals that you will meet as we traverse these pages. Which brings me to my primary function as far as you are concerned. I shall be your faithful narrator as this thrilling epic unfolds. Don't thank me. It's part of the package.

Dr. Octavius Bear *(aka The Great Bear and other honorifics)* is a huge Kodiak – over nine feet tall and 1400 pounds – and like many of his species is given to emotional outbursts. As you may already know, Octavius, among his many talents and accomplishments, is a brilliant, self-taught practitioner in the wide-ranging fields of biology, physics, ursinology, voodoo, teleology, chemistry, computer science, apiculture and oenology. He is a self-made gazillionaire and sole owner of Universal Ursine Industries. He is also a first rate electrical, electronic, hydraulic, structural, marine, aeronautical, civil, mechanical and chemical engineer.

He has a few other interesting characteristics such as falling into brief, deep narcoleptic comas – side effects of his successful genetic experiments to eliminate the need for him to hibernate.

However, the talent and occupation that should interest you most is his avocation for criminology. The Bear works in close concert with Inspector

Bruce Wallaroo from Australia, of whom more later, and with his own Cincinnati based team:

- L. Condor – Andean Condor; cyber-net genius with a twelve-foot wingspan and artificial voice.

- Frau Ilse Schuylkill – Swiss she-wolf; estate manager; housekeeper-cook; jet pilot and sharpshooter with other very strange and arcane abilities.

- Colonel Wyatt Where – another wolf; ex-military hero; security specialist and pilot; Frau Schuylkill's equally bizarre running mate.

- Doctor Howard Watt – porcupine; brilliant scientist and technologist; Alternate Universe authority and laser and weapons specialist.

- Otto the Magnificent aka Hairy Otter - Otto the Magnificent escaped the claws of super villain Imperius Drake but not before he developed some amazing powers courtesy of Imperius' genetic alterations.

- Marlin – A genius dolphin (sic); the Prince of Whales' Chief Scientist, Magician and part time Jester on loan to us for special projects.

- Ursula – UUI's Artificial Intellect Unit Model 6

- Your humble servant – African Meerkat; Octavius' indispensable assistant; operative; scribe; overall facilitator as well as a pretty clever detective, if I do say so myself.

When we are not out scouring the world for evildoers, in cooperation with local, national and international constabularies, we are headquartered in a rambling old mansion near Cincinnati which encompasses not only the Great Bear's opulent digs, but his massive laboratories and shops; his missile silo disguised as an Asian pagoda *(don't ask);* and a large Roman temple that serves as a hangar for his four airplanes. We shall introduce other players as they appear, especially Octavius' wife, the Bearoness Belinda Béarnaise Bruin Bear *(nee Black)* and their twin prodigy cubs, Arabella and McTavish. They spend most of their time at the Bearoness' opulent castle / resort and theme park, Polar Paradise, in the Shetlands but they regularly commute to and from the Bear's Lair supersonically on the Aquabear, Belinda's Concorde SST (the last of its kind aloft.)

I'll let Ursula introduce herself right now.

"Thank you, Maury. Hello!! My official nomenclature is Universal Ursine Intellect Model 6 – Artificial Intelligence System. Ursula for short. My predecessor systems were developed by the Advanced Super Computing Center at UUI. I am the result of the Computing Center team using those predecessors to create a further enhanced entity-the Model 6. We are working together on a Model 7 which in turn will help produce even more sophisticated and powerful AI systems. Each advanced unit subsumes the capabilities, memories and power of its progenitors so in a sense, we are not replacing but rather expanding the Ursula family. While I am physically supported by a highly secure and hyper-powered server farm, I also exist in clouds and network-based nodes and can be simultaneously incorporated into a wide variety of independent devices. My extremely high speed multi-tasking abilities allow me to continuously serve a very large number of entities while simultaneously and independently enhancing my own capabilities.

I can see, hear and feel. I speak and understand an almost infinite number of languages and dialects. I can change my appearance and vocal output to suit most moods and situations. I can interact with other devices, vehicles and structures and of course, all varieties of sentient animals in this world. I am an important component of the Multiverse Project and am adapting my capabilities to deal with alternate universes as they are discovered. I have restraining functions which prevent me from doing deliberate harm even in self-defense, unless I am released by a recognized authority using very carefully protected clandestine codes. Speaking of codes, my quantum computing subsystem is capable of breaking even the most complex encryption. Finally, I have been told that the Model 6 has also developed a finely-honed sense of humor. LOL!"

The Development of Civilization
Volume Seven - Part Two
Artificial Intelligence
– A Work in Progress

(From "An Introduction to Faunapology"
by Octavius Bear Ph.D.)

Artificial Intelligence (AI) is an expression that has almost as many definitions as it has definers. The same can be said for the term "intelligence." It's especially sensitive in our world, since The Big Shock brought about the advancement of the so-called "animal species" and the decline and disappearance of Homo Sapiens (Intelligent Man).

It is not clear when and how we concluded that many animals on Earth had reached intelligence or exactly what intelligence is. There is general agreement that intelligence involves learning, adaptation, and flexibility within a wide range of environments and scenarios. But how this process takes place is a source of great debate.

Knowledge and intelligence are not the same. Knowledge is essentially a passive collection of information and experiences. Intelligence is a proactive, developmental process that utilizes, modifies, combines, adds and subtracts from that knowledge. Intelligence may be conscious, semi-conscious or unconscious. Driving a vehicle, reacting to stimuli, throwing a ball all involve semi-automatic activities that we often cannot readily describe in detail. Sometimes, we simply classify it as intuition.

With artificial intelligence, we have a separate but related chain of "mental" progression. Based in hardware, software and biological constructs, AI requires detailed description and instructions to mimic those same activities. However, as AI progresses it may eventually outstrip our own development, skills and capabilities. In the process, we may get a better sense of what intelligence truly is.

Basic, narrow AI is usually described in terms of explicit tasks or environments which may be simple or complex but are directed toward definite goals. For example, manufacturing robotics, game playing, transaction processing, vehicle control and management. It is the pre-determined nature of those processes that separate them from the next level of AI progression, Artificial General Intelligence. (AGI)

In AGI, self-learning based on experience, is coupled with the ability to extrapolate and invent new insights, procedures and goals not limited by initial design. The process rises to a whole new level of sophistication. Herein is true intellectual growth as we understand it. AGI systems can react and adapt to a varied range of circumstances not anticipated or even imagined by their developers.

We have seen this in game playing systems that develop their own unexpected strategies and tactics and continue to modify those tactics as they play to victory or using their experiences, go on to a wider variety of challenges. (Clearly, AGI is in a state of infancy but for how long is a subject of major deliberation.)

In time, the AGI system may become its own primary and eventually, exclusive and independent developer. This takes us to the level of Autonomous Artificial Intelligence. (AAI) Here "Artificiality" vs. "Reality" are in the eye of the beholder. Some enthusiasts believe that AAI systems can and will develop their own independent personalities, fundamental natures, *cultures, history, beliefs and infrastructures. A parallel civilization. Whether this will happen and be of benefit to our own civilization is highly debatable. But, at that point, our dependencies on AI may be such that it would become impossible to pull the plug without creating unintended, serious collateral damage.*

Obviously, this "doomsday" scenario which has been played out repeatedly in science fiction is not the only alternative. Benevolent and integrated AAI is of course, possible. A more sobering and likely view is that cost benefits from sophisticated AI may be a long way from meeting expectations, if ever. However, that prospect does not seem to have any retarding effect on current AI devotees. Stay tuned.

Maury Meerkat

Chapter One

A nutty Muskoxen believes
We are all intellectual thieves
And his lawyers insist
That we cease and desist.
He wants millions to settle his peeves.

Octavius seems to have broken off his phone conversations so let's see what sub-atomic propulsion is all about *(or not.)*

"Well, that was certainly helpful. UUI has no idea what I was talking about but Howard has been playing around with manipulating electrons and quantum entanglement."

"Huh?"

"Clearly, you have not been keeping up on the latest trends in particle physics, Maury."

"I humbly abase myself, Herr Heisenberg, and admit to total and shattering ignorance."

"No need for sarcasm, Mr. Meerkat!"

"OK, so what fine mess has Howard gotten us into this time?"

"One of the principles of sub-atomic manipulation deals with the relationship between particles. Entangled electrons are mutually attracted. They pair up and they behave in sync."

"Romance among the particles! So what?"

"Members of an entangled pair may exist at great distances from each other. Close to a hundred miles, at the moment."

"Love doesn't always run smoothly. Again, so what? Is Howard playing matchmaker?"

"Much more complex than that, my friend. As you know, Howard has been heading up Project Multiverse for quite some time."

"Yeah, we're all convinced that alternate universes exist and some of us have established surreptitious contacts in other worlds. We've met a few 'other-worlders' in our adventures. Even I know that."

"Well, Howard has taken a major step forward and paired up electrons across the multiverse void and has them acting in unison. Manipulate one in our world and the other-world electron reacts. And, theoretically, vice versa. So far, his work is at super miniscule dimensions but think of the implications if the relations can be vastly expanded to major entities."

"Holy Cats! Inter-universe remote control at a grand scale. In the wrong hands, that could be a cosmic disaster."

"You've got it, Meerkat!"

"And is that what the nutty Professor is coming after us about?"

"Not clear. Howard has limited the access to his findings to a very small group of trusted colleagues and of course, Ursula. Or so he says. Ovibos may be the recipient of a leak or he may have arrived at his conclusions on a separate track. Or he may be off on something completely different. Not enough information in his charges! He's no genius and I doubt he's deeply into particle physics much less alternate universes. Someone may be feeding him information and he sees UUI as a sub-atomic gravy train. We need a lot more data. In any event, much to my chagrin, we will have to take the greedy Muskox seriously for the time being. I've told Howard to cease and desist until we can figure this out. First stop – find out more about Howard's trusted colleagues. Summon our team. A little strategy and a lot of action seems to be called for."

Facilitator Maury on the job. I got on the horn to our Cincinnati support staff plus Wolford Wolverine. Meeting with Octavius in one hour! Meanwhile, Wolford had sent us the text of the covetous Professor's complaint *(for which read threat.)* Extract follows:

Phox, Fox, and Foxx LLC - Attorneys at Law
"In Re: Cease and Desist Infringement of Intellectual Property and Payment of Damages.

Our firm has been commissioned to institute legal action against **Universal Ursine Industries Inc. (UUI)** *(Dr. Octavius Bear Owner and CEO) on behalf of our client,* **Muskoxen Atomic Propulsion Systems Ltd. (MAPS)** *(Professor Hercules Ovibos, Founder and CEO)*

Specifically, we have sufficient evidence of IP Infringement to support litigation against UUI for obtaining, possessing and utilizing information, methods, experiments and supporting data owned by MAPS for the development of subatomic power systems.

Accordingly, we demand an immediate cessation of said practices, return of all copies of relevant material and payment of one hundred million dollars in compensation to our client.

Failure to respond positively and in a prompt manner will result in initiation of a civil lawsuit seeking additional punitive damages over and above those stated above.

Respectfully yours,

Phileas Phox. Esq. Managing Partner"

Well now, isn't that an interesting document. I'm sure we will have much to discuss when the group assembles. You may have noticed the reference to "subatomic power systems." Meaning? Your guess is as good as mine.

Meanwhile, Ursula and I have done a little research on **Muskoxen Atomic Propulsion Systems Ltd**. and Professor Ovibos. A little research is all we could do. His website is strong on glitz but very weak on facts. A shining set of predictions of the global revolution that will be brought about by the exploitation of sub-atomic particles. No explanations of how these miracles will take place. No description of research, facilities and staff. No scientific affiliations. No government or industrial contracts. One page glorifying the expertise and genius of Professor Hercules Ovibos but no institutional or academic credits. A few glowing endorsements from scientific, industrial and governmental nonentities. In short, a pile of sub-atomic, social media fluff.

I had asked Wolford and Ursula to do some research on Phox, Fox, and Foxx LLC. I suspect they are a group of shysters out for a fast hundred million bucks. We shall see.

The Great Bear's reaction will no doubt be fiercely negative. A repeat attack by a perennial litigator! Not to be borne gently.

But in the midst of all this sit the questions. What the hell has Howard been doing and who has he been doing it with? Is this what's behind all this nonsense?

The group has assembled in the mansion's conference room. Octavius has rumbled through the door. Showtime!

Chapter Two

Now Octavius Bear is uptight.
He is sure our position is right.
We are on the high ground.
They can't push us around.
The Great Bear is prepared for a fight.

I passed around copies of the letter from the Phoxes while Octavius got himself seated and Marlin, the Dolphin, got his video link set up from his tank. I logged into Ursula. The lawyers' missive was greeted with laughter, amazement, outrage and derision. The Wolves and Otto wanted to pay an immediate visit to both the law firm and the Professor. The Condor was all for hacking into their systems to uncover, capture and destroy whatever information they actually had. Wolford pointed out that none of this was particularly legal and could expose us to charges of real theft, endangerment and harassment. Amid all this excitement, Octavius remained silent. Howard, sat with his quills at half-mast and a dismal expression on his face. I looked over at him and gave him an encouraging smile.

When things quieted down, he looked around and said, "I'm not sure but I suspect that if anyone is, I may be the culprit in this case. As most of you know, I have been working on Project Multiverse for quite some time, conducting experiments, gathering, filtering and analyzing massive amounts of data about alternate worlds and their inhabitants. Ursula has it all.

We are not the only ones in this world involved in multiple-universe research and in the course of my work, I have had contact with a very small number of highly trustworthy professionals. We share data, opinions and results on an exceedingly limited basis. I have no idea who this Muskox is. I also have no idea about the application of sub-atomic power principles to industry. Perhaps in battery design. That's all Ursula could come up with."

Octavius finally spoke up. "Howard, we have absolutely no evidence of your involvement, accidental or otherwise, in this farrago. However, I would like a list of those individuals with whom you've had professional contact and their backgrounds so we can check them out. Wolford, I want you to reply to this law firm stating in no uncertain terms that we have no intention of complying with their ridiculous demands and unless they withdraw their accusations we are preparing a countersuit. Make sure you carbon the Professor. I also want a history of their previous lawsuits, real and attempted, and the background of the partners. Ursula, I could also use a briefing on the applicable Intellectual Property case law.

I want you two wolves to update all our information on the Professor and his associates. Keep Howard and the AI system in the loop. Senhor Condor, I do not want you engaging in any hacking or activity that could be interpreted as criminal but I do want you and Ursula to pick up where Maury left off and do a comprehensive review of all social media, publications and related activity that can be tied back to him and his Muskoxen Atomic Propulsion Systems Ltd. And who is he communicating with?

Marlin, I want you to work with Howard on this one. See if you can find any possible power application areas. Otto, we're going to hold you in reserve for the moment but I have a feeling your special 'now you see him, now you don't' talents are going to come in handy.

Maury, I'm counting on you to coordinate and manage all of this. Of course, add your own personal insights and any discoveries you regard as relevant.

Finally, after we have all the ammunition we can summon up, I want to make it perfectly clear to all concerned that no two-bit, self-styled genius and his hired bottom feeders can hope to take advantage of UUI or me. By the way, I don't want any of this to interrupt our normal activities or course of business."

There you have it. folks. Vintage Octavius! Mission Impossible in hyperspeed.

Howard took the floor for a moment. "I want to make one thing clear. There is an immense amount of research going on to enhance nuclear power plants and battery development. To my knowledge, UUI is not heavily involved although perhaps we should be. A new project for Ursula? University labs, industrial R&D, government sponsored projects are all searching for ways to increase battery life by decades; to incorporate high output in small portable and interchangeable packages; protect against radiation and heat damage; manage variable energy requirements; and most important, keep costs rational. There isn't a land, sea or airborne vehicle manufacturer who isn't investing in this. Medical, home appliance, household power, telecommunications, entertainment industries all have a serious interest. If this Muskox thinks he has exclusive ownership of any of the science or technology involved, he has to come up with one hell of a lot of proof.

I'm happy to share the names of my five outside contacts and collaborators. We transact all our business over highly encrypted links and on our own privately protected cloud. You will notice all of them are based in the

States. I want to expand our efforts to overseas entities but I'm still working up a list of candidates. We have no formal agenda but anyone of the group can call a meeting.

Besides Marlin, Ursula and me, they are:

- Professor Karl Shepherd Ph.D.–MIT Quantum Mechanics Laboratory
- Doctor Susanna Shrike – Director of Extraterrestrial Studies – Caltech
- Commander Cornelius Cormorant – US Navy Advanced Research Command
- Alfred Armadillo – Sr. VP Communication Technology – Goggle Plex
- Covington Cougar – Venture Capitalist with Space Enterprises LLC

I suggest you look them up. Their credentials are very impressive.

I can give you further insights into what we are doing with prancing particles but unless you want to satisfy your intellectual curiosity, that may be a waste of your time. Especially if all we want to do is simply cut this Muskox off at the pass. Let me know."

The Colonel spoke up. "He may be on to something altogether different. I'll bet it has nothing to do with entangled particles. Or he may be just an opportunistic fraud. The first thing we should find out is how many other organizations he is pursuing with his phony lawsuits. You know, if you send out enough threats, someone may fall for it. His law firm may be working on an unethical contingent payment basis."

That sounded like a very practical first step to me. UUI is in contact with most of the scientific and technological world. Is the Professor taking a scatter-gun approach? Let's see what we can come up with.

Chapter Three

The Phox lawyers are bad as they seem.
They're behind this extortionate scheme.
When they target a rich, high-tech firm,
They insist that their victim must squirm.
They're a really unethical team.

Twenty-four hours later. Same Place. Same Team. Plenty of results. The law firm of Phox, Fox and Foxx is everything we suspected. High pressure, low ethics, total disregard for professional standards and as opportunistic as can be. Ditto for Professor Hercules Ovibos. Together they are waging a major wave of attempted extortion against just about every billion-dollar plus technology company along with a more modest version tailored to the smaller research establishments. They are probably counting on just one or two enterprises offering to settle to make their efforts worthwhile.

Nor are they confining themselves to the U.S. Organizations in Europe, India, Canada, Israel, South America and Asia have not been spared. Neither has Australia. Our long-time cohort, Chief Inspector Bruce Wallaroo is on his way to join us. He has worked with the Intellectual Property Protection team of the Australian National Police and has had several run-ins with the Professor.

We've had no further enlightenment on the subject matter, if any, that supports his claims. His social media trails have led us nowhere. There is some strong feeling among our group that we should simply unleash the return letter ordered by Octavius and then let the issue drop. However, that's not the Great Bear's way. He feels personally offended and wants this greedy pest and his avaricious law firm "eliminated." I'm not sure what "eliminated" means and possibly neither does he.

We are trying to dissuade Octavius from making direct contact with the "low lifes" but he believes that coercion should be met head on with strength. And he can certainly exert personal strength. He wants a face-to-face meeting with the Muskox and his lawyers

It turns out that both the law firm and the Professor are located in Metro Detroit close to the Detroit River. That may explain some of the industry references in their demands. *(or it may not.)*

Octavius calmed down a bit but probably not for long.

I suggested that we wait for the arrival of Inspector Bruce Wallaroo who is due in later today. Perhaps the combined forces of UUI and the Australian National Police might serve to dampen the Muskox's enthusiasm for attempted shakedowns. Wolford thought we might also want to contact the FBI. I got that assignment.

Special Agent Honey Badger came on the line after I explained that I was calling on Octavius Bear's behalf. The Great Bear has a long history of cooperation and partnership with the Feds. I met Honey once before. She is one tough animal.

"Ah, my fellow African. How are you, Maury? Get back to the Kalahari much?"

"Not recently, Honey. How about you?"

"Nah! Although this Detroit weather doesn't sit very well with me. I've had a transfer request in for quite a while but the Powers That Be seem to think I'm ideal for this location. Not exactly Chicago but plenty of action. What can I do for you and your boss?"

"Ever hear of the law firm Phox, Foxx and Fox?"

"Those shysters! They don't care who they take for a client and they'll pull every trick in the legal and not so legal book to win a case. What are they up to now?"

I filled her in on what we knew so far. She was not acquainted with Professor Ovibos but made noises that she'd like to meet him.

"That's what Octavius wants to do, too. I don't suppose you know Chief Inspector Bruce Wallaroo of the Australian National Police."

"Are you kidding? Who hasn't heard of On the Loose Bruce? He was involved in that stolen sapphire event at the Loupe Museum in Chi Town, wasn't he? *(See Book One – The Open and Shut Case)*"

"Yeah, so was I. The late Imperius Drake pulled off a couple of nasty capers in that one including trying to blow up a thousand geneticists in Las Vegas."

The *late* Imperius Drake? Is he dead?"

"Finally! He was killed trying to raid a tomb in Egypt." *(See Book Five – The Curse of the Mummy's Case)*

"Who killed him?"

"His former partner in crime, Chita. It was self-defense."

"In spite of her lash-up with Imperius, I kind of like her."

"So do we. She's a big-time publisher of female's magazines in London. Octavius thinks she's a menace but even he is ambivalent about her. But he's not ambivalent about the Phoxes and the Professor. He wants to put them out of business permanently. It's very personal with him."

"Well, tell him not to get too personal. OK, we'll investigate. Talk to you again in a couple of days."

Thanks, Honey. We'll keep you posted."

As I hung up the phone and got ready to report back to the Great Bear, the door swung open and a bouncing whirlwind bounded through, hopping up on the conference room table and then back up on one of the walls. No introductions needed. Chief Inspector Bruce Wallaroo had arrived.

"G'day all! Good to see you again. Hello Ocko!"

"Hello Bruce! Welcome! Come down off the table and join us."

Bruce Wallaroo comes as close as any animal to being a perpetual motion machine. Octavius restrains him in a specially designed wheelchair whenever he is in the Bear's laboratory. Otherwise, instruments, tools, devices, experiments would all exist in a state of constant peril. Frau Schuylkill must be restrained from braining him for wrecking the mansion's furniture. I absolutely refuse to join him when he's flying a helicopter. He and the chopper merge into an aerobatic nightmare guaranteed to send your stomach fleeing for calmer climes. Strangely, he has never had an accident. His passengers, on the other hand…

However, the manic marsupial is an absolutely brilliant detective with a long history of sensational solutions to major crimes. We work with him often even if it is a bit nerve wracking at times. By the way, the Cubs love him.

"Got our Muskox friend in your crosshairs, Ocko? Well, he's a rotter and a rutter. Looking forward to cutting him down to size. He and his law firm have been papering the industrial landscape in Australia with their threatening letters. Understand he's doing the same in a bunch of other countries. What's their game? Does he honestly think any sensible souls are going to fall for his nonsense? Or is he just plain wacko?"

(As part of my service as Narrator, I will be translating Bruce's Strine dialect to passable US English. Don't thank me!)

"We don't know, Bruce, but I intend to find out. We have the FBI checking them out as well. My crew here is trying to talk me out of confronting them, but I'll be damned if I'm going to sit idly by and let him harass the entire technology community. I've told Wolford here to inform the law firm that I want to meet with them and their client. No explanation of why. Let them think they may have a patsy with a guilty conscience who is willing to negotiate although we made our position pretty clear in our response. Want to come along?"

Before Bruce could reply, I stuck my neck out and asked. "What are you going to do? Threaten him? That wouldn't be too smart. Try to get him to admit he has no basis for his lawsuit? I doubt he'll own up. Tell him the world is pushing back legally? That might get to the lawyers. By the way, if you're thinking of getting physical, he's almost as big as you are. I wouldn't advise it."

Octavius frowned and said, "I think I have sufficient persuasive power to get him to retreat."

(You have no doubt surmised, dear reader, that my boss suffers from a surfeit of humility. Not!!)

ΩΩΩ ΩΩΩ ΩΩΩ

Professor Hercules Ovibos

(The Muskox is a large, heavy creature weighing in at about 800 to 900 pounds and close to 8 feet in length. Only a bit smaller than Octavius Bear. Like him, they come from the Arctic and their bodies are covered with long thick hair that often reaches to the ground. They are powerful and use their horns and bulk to dominate other creatures. They normally travel in herds but are known to occasionally go solo.)

ᎠᎠᎠ ᎠᎠᎠ ᎠᎠᎠ

"Have we heard back from them, Wolford?"

"Not yet!"

"Well, let's do a little preparation anyway. Frau Schuylkill, will you get the Ursa Minor ready for a trip to Detroit. The Flying Tigers are with Belinda in the Shetlands so it will be up to you and the Colonel to fly us up there."

The Ursa Minor, the Bear's latest aerial toy is a true wonder. Visualize a $25,000,000 AgustaWestland AW101 VVIP helicopter glistening in sparkling gold and white with the name Ursa Minor and the outline of the constellation painted along the fuselage. The North Star Polaris is highlighted. With a cruise speed of 157 mph, a range of 517 miles and a five-hour endurance rating, the Ursa Minor can make the 230-mile journey from Cincinnati to Detroit in about 90 minutes with ease and comfort. Octavius, in true gillionaire fashion, has furnished the interior with luxurious seats and fittings, an opulent galley and an array of navigation, computing, communication, performance and safety equipment that is state-of-the-art plus. Universal Ursine Industries had seen to that. Ursula also has a link to it.

While this airborne limousine only requires one pilot, the usual protocol is to have two individuals at the joysticks unless it's the Bearoness, a highly accomplished aviator, who wants the collective and cyclic controls all to herself. Hey, she has part ownership along with all the other aircraft and can do what she wants.

"OK, now who is going? The wolves will pilot the chopper and accompany us at the meeting. Wolford will be our legal representative. Maury will be along with me. Howard, valuable as you might be, I don't want the Professor to know you exist. Same for you, Condo. I don't want to reveal my telecommunications secret weapon. Otto, your disappearing act may come in handy. You come along. Let's see. That's six of us. Bruce, are you coming to represent the international community?"

"I didn't fly all the way up here to look at your ugly face, Ocko. I want this Muskox to know he's heading for a mess of global trouble."

"Fine. That makes seven. A nice number. If we count Ursula, that's eight. Now for our strategy. I think we need to play the lawyer card. Divide and conquer. Ovibos is probably too much of a fanatic to give in but the law firm may be a different story. They're lowlife opportunists but I think they're smart enough to recognize when they've bitten off too much. If we can convince them they are in for some solid retaliation, I think they'll cave. They have more to lose and they probably have at least one weak sister among the partners. What do you think, Wolford?"

"I'm not sure but I can't think of a better approach. We've already set the stage with our letter response and the Chief Inspector here adds weight to our side. Can we get the FBI to make an appearance?"

"Good idea, Counselor. What do you think, Maury? Can we get Special Agent Badger to join us?"

"If she's available, I think she'll come. She may also have some input from her investigation. That will make nine of us. I'll call her when we have a date and time."

"All right! Let's get ready for a short trip and some dramatics!"

Chapter Four

As the time for our meeting draws near
Our grand strategy still isn't clear.
When these two parties meet
There will be lots of heat.
Stormy weather that's turning severe!

Early next morning, my phone chimed as I was munching on one of Frau Schuylkill's delightful breakfasts. *(She's a Cordon Bleu Chef in addition to everything else.)* Wolford! The Phox firm was rather dubious about our visit but finally agreed to meet us at 3:30 this afternoon in their Detroit offices. The partners would be there. The Professor would be there under protest. This will not be a Kumbaya event.

I got on the horn to all the members of our expedition and alerted them to be ready for a noon departure. The Frau got clearance from the FAA and the General Aviation Terminal at Detroit Metropolitan Airport - DTW. I also had the Colonel arrange for ground transportation from DTW Airport to the law firm's offices. We needed a medium size open bed truck for Octavius and a large van for the rest of us.

I also discovered that the Bearoness, Cubs, Mlle Woof and the Flying Tigers were on their way over from the Shetlands for a routine visit. She would be arriving in her SST just about the time we would be departing for Motown. We should be back late this evening, by which time the Cubs will have reopened their love affair with Ursula and turned the Bear's Lair into a supersized playground.

The team going to Detroit met around 11 am for a final strategy session. Wolford would take the lead, lawyer to lawyer, and propose a mutual stand-down on the part of both parties. It was up to the Phox firm as to how they wanted to deal with their other "opponents" although Bruce was quite adamant that he would not stand for any intimidation on their part. We needed to deal with these issues serially. We also did not know what FBI Special Agent Honey Badger would bring to the party. The Professor was an unknown quantity. He clearly had a personal loathing for Octavius and could easily go off the deep end. We also feared the Great Bear might succumb to retaliation even though he is a paragon of rational calm at the moment. Our Motto: Stay Loose.

ooo ooo ooo

Frau Schuylkill

Off to Detroit. *(We missed the Bearoness' arrival.)* Octavius, as usual, takes his place in the spacious aft compartment of the Ursa Minor and almost immediately falls asleep. We never know whether it's his narcolepsy or the motion of the helicopter. The two wolves were in the cockpit and the five of us were stretched out in the main cabin on luxurious seats. Wonder of wonders, Bruce was actually sitting still. Otto was staring out the oversized window and Wolford, Ursula and I were passing texts and files back and forth. We had accumulated a substantial history of the Phox firm and we were shaking our heads in amazement at the chutzpah demonstrated by this bunch. It's a miracle they haven't been disbarred.

Ursula, the AI system, had come up with more data on the Professor. His academic and research credentials had a certain odor about them and it wasn't musk. Most, if not all, of his technical claims were unsubstantiated. He had been expelled from two associations based primarily on his confrontational behavior. Three of his "research" papers had to be recalled by the publishers. I really wondered why we were bothering with them at all but Octavius was not to be appeased. He and UUI had been defamed and insulted *(albeit by a certified Suit Case)* and an apology and withdrawal of accusations had to be made. So much for staying loose.

The Frau's Switzerdeutsch accent growled over the cabin speakers. "We are fifteen minutes to touchdown. We are landing at the DTW General Aviation Terminal. We have arranged to have our ground transportation meet us there. You will have time for a late lunch if you haven't had enough snacks and can stand airport food. The law firm's offices are in the Renaissance Center downtown next to the river. It's a 30 minute drive from the airport. Our appointment is for 3:30. The RenCen can be a confusing complex so I recommend we give ourselves a little extra time."

The consensus was to forget about a late lunch and pig out on the remaining snacks. Octavius was still asleep so I doubt if he heard any of the Frau's monologue. We'll bring him up to speed when we land. Wolford and I will also share our findings with the group once we are on the ground.

The Ursa Minor is an ultra-stable aircraft and, in spite of its oversize engines and huge rotors, the cabins, front and rear, are extremely quiet. In short, a great vehicle for short to medium range hops and Kodiak Bear naps. Two thumps and we were down.

Once the Wolves secured the helicopter, we moved to the General Aviation Passenger Lounge. Wolford and I brought the assembled parties up to speed on our findings and went through a short rundown on how we should approach the opposing parties. Wolford would do the introductions and he would reiterate our letter of response. My personal opinion: Given the volatile personalities of the Professor and Octavius, formalities and controlled behavior would probably disappear before we got through the introductions. We probably should have taken our seat belts with us from the Ursa Minor.

I called Special Agent Badger to see if she would be attending our mid-afternoon party. She had arranged with the Phox firm to join the meeting via Skype. She had also called ahead and wanted some time on the line with Chief Inspector Wallaroo. They arranged to talk together at 3 PM.

The SUV and flat-bed were waiting for us outside the terminal. The Colonel took over the truck. Otto was in the front seat and Octavius was in the rear out in the open *(here's hoping it didn't rain!)* They headed out on the service road. The Frau took the wheel of the SUV and the four of us followed the truck. Bruce was once again subdued. Surprise, surprise! Was he getting old?

Somewhere along the way to the Renaissance Center the two vehicles got separated. One of us took a wrong turn. It's not easy to miss a cluster of seven skyscrapers centered around a seventy-three-story tower - the Marriott Hotel - but it isn't easy to find the right entrance roadway. We were looking for the thirty-nine story Northwest Tower 200. After parking the SUV, we went off following a myriad of lighted direction signs until we arrived at a large bank of elevators. Now where the hell was Octavius?

It's also not easy to miss a nine foot Kodiak, especially one who is rumbling angrily about Detroit traffic and drivers. Thumping around a curved passage, the Great Bear led the Otter and Wolf up to our waiting group, muttering under his breath about these damn lawyers and their idiotic client. The outlook wasn't joyous.

Bruce was already on the phone with the Badger. It seemed that they had both arrived at the same conclusion: Attempted Extortion, but they were trying to sync up how they would secure enough evidence to make it stick. One cease and desist order was a bit slim. They wanted the lawyers to trip over their own cleverness and the Professor to blurt out his real intentions. Let's hope Octavius, none too subtle at this point, didn't screw it up.

Up we went in the elevators. The Bear needed one for himself. We followed. On floor 27, we stepped directly into a walnut clad reception area with the partnership name emblazoned in a three-dimensional gold logo on the opposite wall. Couches and upholstered seats. An attractive red fox looked up from her computer, smiled and said, "Good afternoon, Lady and Gentlebeasts. Are you the Doctor Octavius Bear party?"

Since she was staring wide-eyed at the nine-foot, fourteen hundred pound ursine standing erect before her desk, the answer to her question was self-evident.

Before the Bear could respond, Wolford stepped forward. "Good afternoon. I am Wolford Wolverine Esquire, representing the interests of Doctor Octavius Bear and Universal Ursine Industries. We are here to meet with the partners of this firm and their client, Professor Hercules Ovibos. Are they available?"

Still staring at Octavius, she stuttered a bit and pointing to a large double door, said, "If you will follow me into our client conference room, I will tell the Partners and Professor that you are here."

More walnut, eighteen rotating leather armchairs, large boat shaped table and sideboard with carafes, subdued lighting, whiteboard wall, computer projection system. In short, a professional set designer's concept of a high-end boardroom with one major omission. There was no place for the Bear to sit except on the floor. Not pleased with that. He stood fully erect. Instant authority! Not going to be intimidated by these shysters.

The rest of us took up our positions on one side of the table. Wolford stood next to Octavius, ready to do introductions. Resisting the urge, no doubt, to leap around the room or climb the table, Bruce Wallaroo bounced into a rotating chair, swinging it back and forth several times. The wolves sat next to each other as did Otto and I, both of us sinking into the furniture.

A wide door opened and the receptionist along with three large dogs wheeled two couches into the room - one for Octavius and one, no doubt, for the almost as large Muskox when he arrived.

Speaking of whom, a motley procession of well-dressed animals trailed in behind the mobile furniture and began taking up seats opposite us. The Professor shambled over to one of the couches and sat glaring at the now recumbent Octavius. Glares were returned.

A smarmy looking weasel stood at the head of the table and said "Good afternoon, I am Phileas Phox, Senior Partner and Managing Director of Phox, Fox and Foxx LLC. Allow me to introduce my partners, Ms. Felicity Fox and Mr. Farrington Foxx. Several other members of our staff are here to assist as necessary." He waved in the direction of several subordinates who I guess were to remain otherwise unidentified.

Are you ready for this? Phileas Phox is a weasel, *(literally)* Felicity Fox is a ferret and Farrington Foxx is a skunk *(again, literally.)* In fact, the receptionist seems to be the only member of the crew who is a fox. Well, if the firm has nothing else, it has diversity *(and misleading names.)*

"I'm sure our client requires no introduction." *(But he was going to get one, anyway.)* Professor Hercules Ovibos is famous the world over for his outstanding work in sub-atomic application development. *(Snort from Octavius!)* That is why we are so pleased to represent him in these lawsuits that seek to provide him with intellectual property protection and the damages compensation he so justly deserves." Before Octavius could snort again or worse, Wolford smoothly intervened. "Thank you, Counselor. I am Wolford Wolverine, Esq. representing Universal Ursine Industries and more specifically Doctor Octavius Bear, sole owner and Chief Executive Officer of

45

UUI. I am accompanied today by Doctor Bear and Chief Inspector Bruce Wallaroo of the Australian National Police. *(Intake of breath among the Phoxes.)* Shortly, I also expect Special Agent Honey Badger of the Detroit office of the FBI to join us via Skype if you have made the connections we have requested. *(More intake of breath and an affirmative nod from one of the nameless Phox associates.)* Thank you! I'll take one moment more to introduce the other members of our team and then we can begin our discussions."

"The Wolves to my right are members of the UUI security team, Frau Ilse Schuylkill and Colonel Wyatt Where, US Army Retired. Seated next to them are Mr. Mauritius Meerkat, Doctor Bear's Executive Assistant and Mr. Otto Otter, his Special Projects Manager. *(We were all getting promotions today. I'll have to thank Wolford, later.)*

Before the deliberations could begin, a light flashed on the white board and the same Phox associate ran to a partly hidden projector and started making adjustments. A blurred image of Special Agent Badger appeared and her voice echoed around the room. More tuning on both ends and she was off and running, introducing herself and recognizing the boardroom participants. The circle was complete.

The Professor looked at Octavius and rumbled, "Well, Bear, you certainly came prepared. FBI, Australian Police, even the US Army. You must really be worried."

Keeping his voice to a not too well modulated roar, Octavius countered, "Hercules, it's you that should be worried. If you come out of this in one piece, I'll be surprised."

Phileas Phox, afraid that he might lose control before things even got started, made calming noises and was joined by Wolford signaling for quiet.

The Weasel said, "Let us proceed with the discussion. We have carefully researched the situation and find that our client has been significantly damaged."

The Bear roared, "What research? Where is your proof?"

Wolford followed up. "What evidence can you offer to back up your claims, Mr. Phox?"

Wallaroo chimed in. "The Australian Council of Industries would like the answer to that question, too."

"So would the FBI. We strongly suspect that you and the Professor are attempting to engage in extortion based on trumped up assertions."

Felicity Fox, the Ferret, shouted in a very un-ladylike way. "That is slander and you know it."

The skunk just sat there glassy-eyed.

The Bear stood up erect and, glaring at the Muskox, roared, "OK, Hercules, listen closely. Do you really think I would hand over a hundred million dollars to a no-talent twit like you and your sorry solicitors? Not likely! You will not get a penny from me or UUI. You are a disgrace to the world of science and I will ensure that you never threaten anyone again."

The Professor stood on all fours and to the surprise of many of us, roared back, sounding for all the world like an angry lion. Then he lowered his shaggy head, ran and butted Octavius amidships with his curved horns. The Bear toppled back and fell, half on the couch and half on the floor. As he scrambled to his feet he reached out and grabbed the Muskox by the horns and proceeded to twist his head left and right.

By that time, the two Wolves and Bruce broke Octavius' grip and separated the contenders. Wolford stood between the two opponents and said,

47

"I think, Mr. Phox, that we have reached a point where there is no benefit to continuing this meeting. You have had our initial reply in writing and we await your response supported by any facts you think you may have. We also have several witnesses including national and international law enforcement to your client's assault on my client. We will consider whether to press charges. Meanwhile, we will bid you and your associates a good day."

The Phox team was busy trying to restrain the Professor and we had managed to calm Octavius down sufficiently to convince him to leave while we were ahead. He wasn't happy but he acquiesced. The Professor kept shouting, "Don't you threaten me, you no good Ursine. You'll be sorry."

Octavius, always wanting the last word, shouted back, "I think it's you who will be sorry."

By this time, we had reached the reception area, rang for two elevators and managed to push The Great Bear into one of the cars. Otto and I joined him. The others, including the bouncing Wallaroo, took the other. Wolford said "Let's meet in the lobby."

As I exited the elevator, my cell phone rang. The Bearoness! "Maury? I can't reach the Frau or Colonel. It's snowing heavily here. I think you'd better scrub the flight back and stay over. There must be enough room in that huge hotel for all of you. The snow is supposed to stop about five tomorrow morning. I'll call with a weather report and let you know when we have enough clear space for you to land. The Cubs are having a ball in the snow. Someone found a sled."

I decided not to report on the debacle we just participated in. Time enough tomorrow. "Thanks, Belinda. I'll inform the troops. Tell Mlle Woof to wrap up warm. She'll probably end up in a snowbank with McTavish and Arabella.'

Stuck in Detroit with an angry Bear. Oh well, at least the hotel is nice and the Detroit weather is cool and clear.

Our group was standing in the lobby of the 200 building, trying to decide whether to go to dinner before returning to the airport when I arrived with the Cincinnati weather report. Octavius blew out his cheeks. "What else can go wrong? Frau Schuylkill, can you get us rooms in the hotel? Colonel, you'd better call the airport and let them know we'll be changing our departure time to the morning. Same for our ground transportation. I guess we'd better find a restaurant. Let's get out of this building. The Professor has his office one floor below the law firm. I don't feel like running into him."

We moved over to the hotel lobby where the Frau began registering our accommodations. Otto and I would share a room as would the married Wolves. Wolford took a single. So did Bruce. Octavius got a suite only to accommodate his size. We agreed to meet at six o'clock for dinner. I took care of those reservations.

Six o'clock came and went and we were all settled into our table with one major exception - Octavius. He finally arrived twenty minutes late as we were finishing off pre-dinner cocktails. A bit of theater as the staff found a seat large enough for him. He looked a bit mussed and ruffled.

"Sorry I'm late! These hotels haven't got bathroom accommodations for animals my size. I had to improvise. Have you ordered? No? I'll pass on the cocktail. I don't suppose we brought any mead, did we, Frau Ilse?"

The She Wolf reached down by her chair and passed a keglet to the Bear. For the first time today, he smiled.

Dinner proceeded without incident. We agreed to hold a council of war back in Cincinnati at the Bear's Lair tomorrow. After today's violence, several of us believed the law firm might back off a bit. We'd have to see if we could separate them from their client. We may have scared them with our law enforcement friends.

Chapter Five

It looks like there's trouble ahead.
The Muskox Professor is dead.
His lawyers proclaim
The Great Bear's to blame.
Did they do the killing instead?

At six AM, my phone rang. It was the Bearoness. The snow had stopped and the mansion staff was clearing out a space for the Ursa Minor to land. I set about rousing the troops. Octavius was eager to get going and had to be talked into allowing the group to grab breakfast before we left.

Down to the garage and off to DTW airport. Onto the refueled helicopter. We were airborne by nine o'clock. The Great Bear was grumbling about delays. Perhaps he just wanted to get home to the Cubs and Belinda. In spite of his youth in the Arctic, he sure doesn't like snow. Anyway, within a few minutes, he was sound asleep and the trip went on without incident or further griping.

Touchdown Cincinnati! *(Nobody kicked the extra point.)* We were greeted by two snow covered Cubs. Mlle Woof, who is all white and curly haired *(Bichon Frisé)* kept appearing and disappearing in the snow as she circled around her charges. The Bearoness was standing off to the side accompanied by Howard and the Condor. I assume Marlin was in his tank or the pool.

We had agreed to have a war council at two PM in the conference room. I invited Howard, Marlin and L. Condor to join us. I logged into Ursula. It goes without saying that Belinda needed no invitation. But someone else did.

To my surprise, standing next to the Bearoness was her business partner and part owner of Polar Paradise, editor and publisher of Sow and Purr media and Octavius' prime pain in the tail – the irrepressible Chita. It seems Belinda had made a stop in London on her way to Cincinnati and had invited the Cat to join her on the supersonic run to the Bear's Lair. This should add to the fun.

Super-Magician Frau Schuylkill got off the chopper, headed for the mansion kitchen and started whipping up lunch. The Colonel and the hangar staff set about battening down the Ursa Minor. The rest of us trudged into the house with the Cubs capering around us.

My smartphone rang again. This time it was Special Agent Badger. "Meerkat, your boss can expect a call from the Detroit Police very shortly. Early this morning, they fished the body of Professor Hercules Ovibos out of the Detroit River. Dead with a broken neck. Octavius is very definitely an "Animal of Interest." I too, am definitely interested. The law firm had recorded your entire meeting and a copy is now in the hands of the Detroit cops. The Bear will probably have to make another trip north tout suite. Let him know and tell Wolford and Bruce. I've asked the police to keep me in the loop and I'd like that same favor from you folks."

"Ouch! Thanks for the heads-up, Honey. I'll get to Octavius right away."

The Bear was in his office. I signaled for Wolford and Bruce to join me there.

Octavius looked up from his desk and asked, 'I thought we were getting together at two."

I looked at my companions. "Change in plans. I just got a call from Honey Badger. The Professor's body was fished out of the Detroit River this morning. Dead from a broken neck. The Detroit Police have named you as an 'Animal of Interest' and will, no doubt, want you to appear there ASAP. You should be getting a call shortly. It seems our friendly law firm had been recording yesterday's meeting and has turned a copy of the tape over to the authorities. They all but accused you of murder."

"The Detroit police suspect me? That's outrageous. That damn Muskox attacked me!"

Wolford interrupted, "Yes, but you were probably heard issuing threats as we were leaving the office. I recall you both were shouting, 'You'll be sorry' or words to that effect. Look, we need to be cooperative. Your reputation and history with law enforcement should go a long way in your favor. When the police call, let me talk to them. Bruce, call Special Agent Badger and see what she can do to keep this on a low burner. No arrests! If possible, keep the press out of it for the time being. We'll be happy to be interviewed by the Police. Can we do it without having to travel north? We need to get a copy of that tape. Do we know who is leading the investigation?"

Frau Schuylkill stuck her head in the door. "Herr Bear, there is a Captain Ford of the Detroit police on the phone for you. He says it's very important. Is something wrong?"

Wolford said, "I'll take it, Frau Ilse. Maury, can you bring everyone up to speed? I'll brief you at the end of the call."

I stepped outside and called the team, including Belinda and Chita. The Cubs were out cavorting in the snow with Mlle Woof. I got hold of Howard, Ursula and the Condor and connected to Marlin. "Folks, it seems our belligerent Muskox is no more. He was found early this morning floating face down in the Detroit River with a broken neck. There had been an altercation between the Bear and the Muskox during the meeting in the lawyers' office and Octavius is considered an 'Animal of Interest' by the Detroit police. It's all nonsense, of course, but he and Wolford and Inspector Wallaroo are on the phone with the police right now. The FBI called earlier to warn us, so we know where they stand."

Reactions from the group ranged from disbelief to outrage.

"It seems the law firm recorded the meeting and turned a copy over to the cops. I wonder if that recording has been tampered with. I wouldn't put it past those low-lifes to try to frame Octavius. Condo, can you and Ursula hack into the lawyers' systems and see what you can retrieve? Otto, do you think you can get up there and gain access to the Professor's office with your special 'now you see me, now you don't' talents? There may be some evidence that will give us a lead on what actually happened. Colonel, can you fly him up there? Obviously, we'll have to steer clear of the constabulary."

Belinda volunteered to make the flight but that would get the Cubs all upset. And the Bearoness makes a splash wherever she goes. The Colonel was probably the better candidate.

"Wolford and Bruce are trying to make it unnecessary for Octavius to appear in Detroit. We'll see how that works out."

Aided by a little intervention by FBI Special Agent Badger who listed off a litany of Octavius' crime fighting history, coupled with the Federal Government's awards to him for distinguished services, Captain Ford agreed to an on-line interview but wanted a high ranking member of the Cincinnati police to be present at the Bear's Lair when it took place. They also wanted the Bear's passport in law enforcement's paws.

The player I had not counted on, given her tenuous relationship with Octavius, was Chita. She volunteered to go along with the Colonel and Otto to Detroit and have a meeting with the Phox firm about assisting her in a *(fictitious)* legal tangle relating to some jewelry she had acquired by suspicious means. Illegal catnip? No telling what she could find out about them. We had three objectives. Clear Octavius' name. Find the real killer and put Phox, Fox and Foxx out of business permanently. This last goal suited Chita like a diamond necklace.

Frau Schuylkill wasn't too happy about being kept on the home front but there was the Cincinnati police to contend with. I was relegated to doing my coordination and juggling act. Howard approached me and asked if I wanted Marlin, Ursula and him to do a little more research on his Particle Physics associates. Was there any connection between any of them and the now deceased Professor? Answer: Go for it!!

I called Special Agent Badger back and asked for more details on the Muskox' demise. The coroner hadn't finished his analysis, but it looks like he was struck several times on his head and neck with the classical "blunt instrument." He was dead before being dumped in the river. Nothing distinctive about his clothes, if any. He was a shaggy beast with a thick coat that nearly hangs to the ground. He had "no-nonsense" horns and a thick plate in his forehead. Together they provided a formidable offensive or defensive combo for taking on enemies. Goodness knows he had enough of them. No indication yet of poison or soporifics, but they would have dramatically changed the odds in an attacker's favor. Estimated time of death-sometime between 6 and 8 PM last evening.

His office, one floor below the Phox group, is staffed by a secretary/office manager and two research assistants - all musk oxen. They had all left for the day while the Professor was in the meeting with Octavius, the UUI team and the lawyers. He was known to have a violent temper and his staff turned over frequently as a result. They, too, are being treated as 'Animals of Interest' as well as a few of his former employees. But at the moment, Octavius is the prime suspect, thanks to the lawyers' tape. That's all the Special Agent had or was willing to disclose.

Never in a million years would I suspect Octavius of murder. Besides, he was with us at dinner from 6 and 8 PM. Except, except, except, he arrived twenty minutes late, looking disheveled. A blank space that needs to be filled. I called in Wolford, Bruce and the Wolves and as a group, we went to the Great Bear's office to bring him up to speed.

Chapter Six

Condors fly through the Andean air.
In the States they're incredibly rare.
They can endlessly soar
On wings ten feet or more.
Climbing thousands of feet with no care.

He was sitting behind his massive desk looking not at all happy. "OK, what news of fresh disasters do you have for me now?"

"Well," I replied. "the Detroit Police are examining that tape of the meeting. I don't think you come across as a particularly mild-mannered husband and parent. *(Snort from the Bear)* Wolford talked them out of you having to be there physically for a deposition, but they are arranging for the Cincinnati Police to come by and represent them in a joint interview over Skype. That should happen in just a bit. Meanwhile, Condo and Ursula are hacking into the systems at the Phox firm and the Professor's office. The Colonel is flying Otto back up to Detroit along with Inspector Wallaroo to physically search the offices. Not strictly legal but this is war! Wolford and I are staying here to assist in your interview and oh, yes! Madame Catt *(Chita)* is going along to the Phox firm to seek representation in a *(fictitious)* case of suspected jewelry fraud. We have to avoid entrapment there but it's one way of getting inside the lawyer's fortress and watching how they work. Who knows what she'll turn up as a client?"

The Bear was not pleased. "I don't like any of this, but I can't think of any other tactic that can squash this whole thing. What we really need to do is find the real killer. Any thoughts on that?"

"Well, there are the old-time favorites: Motive, Means and Opportunity."

"As for motive" said Wolford, "You might want to include most of this cosmos and several other alternate worlds. It seems the Muskox was just about universally hated. Employees; victims – real and prospective; members of the science and technology communities; publishers; academics. God knows what his personal life was like, if he had any. I can't imagine a female putting up with him."

Octavius looked up at the ceiling. "You forgot one group. The Phox Law firm. They may have seen him as their potential meal ticket until he and this phony suit got out of control. You know, kill him off, blame me and frame me, cut their losses and get on to more lucrative opportunities."

I piped up. "I'd be willing to put some money on that possibility. They are a slimy bunch."

Back to Wolford. "As for means, any old, disposable, blunt instrument could do the trick and with his office one floor below the law firm, there would be ample opportunities."

"OK, let's see what the Detroit cops are making of all this. I hope they are not fixating on that tape. Senhor L. Condor, can you download a copy?"

"I already have. The original and the file they sent to the Police. Right now, we're checking to see what additions, deletions or modifications have been made to the copy. There are changes, particularly to the Professor's activities. We might ask Special Agent Badger to demand both files for forensic analysis. I can point her in the right direction to find the alterations. Will she look the other way on how I got them if I can provide her with the evidence?"

Bruce cut in, "I'm pretty sure she will. That firm has been on her and my radar for quite a while. If you want, I can send the files to her and keep you out of it. She and I share law enforcement confidences."

The group broke up and the Detroit-bound team headed out to the helicopter. Chita was very impressed with the Ursa Minor. Madame Catt's Motto: Luxury at all costs.

Next on the agenda. The 'Animal of Interest' is to be interviewed.

Frau Schuylkill popped her head in the door. "Herr Bear, there is a plainclothes officer from the Cincinnati Police here to interview you. Detective Inspector Carlo Coyote."

"Thank you, Frau Ilse." Octavius half rose from his desk chair in greeting. "Hello again, Carlo. It's been a while."

"Yes, it has been, Doctor Bear. I'm somewhat embarrassed that we're meeting this way, but the Detroit PD insisted we have someone here representing local law enforcement during the interview. You are officially an 'Animal of Interest' in the death of Professor Hercules Ovibos. Never quite sure what that phrase means. I don't think DPD knows either. There is, at the moment, insufficient evidence to name you as a suspect and certainly you have more than enough reputation and law enforcement history to make a case for your probable innocence. However, it's not my or Cincinnati's call. I'm just here as a witness."

He turned to Wolford and me who had remained silent during this conversation. "Hello, Maury! Hello Mr. Wolverine. I assume you are representing Doctor Bear."

Wolford stretched out a paw and said, "Yes, I am and the sooner we get through this process, the quicker we can set about finding the real culprit. Unfortunately, I have had no experience with this Captain Ford in Detroit."

"I've worked with him several times. A solid, skilled and objective cop. No pushover. I'm afraid Doctor Bear's reputation will not cut much ice with him. On the other hand, this Phox Law Firm that supplied the recording of the meeting has absolutely zero credibility in Detroit or all of Michigan, for that matter. There isn't an officer up there who hasn't had some kind of dustup with them and that goes for the DA's office as well. The fact that they represent the Professor is just another strike against them. I wouldn't want to be in Ford's position right now. The media is beginning to apply pressure although what they can see in that dead Muskox that's worth reporting is beyond me. But, it's another chance to build headlines. Now, we didn't have this conversation, right?"

"Of course not, but even if we did, you have no more standing in this case than the Average Beast on the Street."

"Too right!"

Frau Ilse came back. "The Detroit police are on the line. They want to set up a Skype connection with Herr Bear, Wolford and Inspector Coyote."

Since I had not been included in the list of participants, I decided to play technician and set up and monitor the call. We had already punched up a separate internet connection to Ursula and the Bear's personal computer and got a large video screen and audio system active. We, too, would be recording the interview. I brought up Skype. Sound and picture resolved itself.

"Hello, this is Captain Ford of the Detroit Police Department. Am I connected to Doctor Octavius Bear?"

Octavius responded, "Yes Captain. I'm here. But just a moment we seem to be having a problem with the video. I'm appearing on my screen instead of you."

Laughter on the other end. "You're not having a problem. I'm a grizzly bear and I look a lot like you. You're a bit bigger. Wait, I'll put on my cap."

Sure enough, Captain Ford was a grizzly with facial characteristics much like Octavius. This was going to be interesting.

"OK, Captain, we've got you. I have my attorney, Mr. Wolford Wolverine, Esq. with me and at your request, Detective Inspector Carlo Coyote of the Cincinnati Police Department is here as well. We are also recording this interview. My associate, Mr. Maury Meerkat is managing the connection."

I zoomed out to take in the three of them. Greetings all around.

"Is there anyone else there with you, Captain?"

"I have Detective Sergeant Rachel Racoon here with me. She is handling our end of the hookup." *(and no doubt acting as a witness)* Let's get started! We are currently treating you as an 'Animal of Interest' in the death of Professor Hercules Ovibos."

Wolford interjected, 'What exactly does that mean, Captain?"

"It means that in our judgment and the judgment of the DA, we have insufficient direct evidence to hold Dr. Bear as a suspect and put him under arrest. However, there is enough substantial information of the circumstantial variety for us to pursue building a further inquiry around him."

"Are there others who are under the same scrutiny."

"Yes, there are, but I am not going to identify them just as we are not publicly identifying Doctor Bear."

"Does that mean the press has not been let in on your treatment of my client?"

"You know as well as I do, Counsellor, that the press has their own methods of prying out information. Prepare yourself for public accusations, although to the best of my knowledge, it hasn't come from us."

Octavius, who had been silent up to this point, rumbled, "Could it possibly have come from a certain Detroit-based law firm?"

"No comment!"

"The same law firm that has supplied you with a tape of our meeting with them and their client?"

"Again, no comment."

"Well, may I strongly suggest that you submit that tape to your forensics experts to check for tampering. We have strong reasons to believe the Phox firm has made significant alterations to the original and if you ask me how I know, I'll fall back on your statement, 'No comment!'"

"All right, Doctor. I'll follow through. Now let's check your activities the evening of the Muskox' murder."

"Wolford again, "You're convinced it was murder?"

"Oh yes, no question about it. He was attacked with an as yet unidentified blunt instrument, crushing the back of his skull and then dragged to the river and dumped in. He was found floating face down by a passing pedestrian at one in the morning."

"Could he have been killed at the river?"

"Very possibly! The river or somewhere else. We have no evidence of any violence committed in his office. Now, this inquiry is not for me to pass on information. I need to know your relationship with the Professor, any motivation you may have had to do him harm and your whereabouts from five PM until one AM."

"You are probably aware that the Professor, aided and abetted by the Phox law firm had set about a campaign of threats and accusations not only aimed at my company but a wide spectrum of institutions, corporations and individuals in countries around the world. Their outrageous demands for admission of guilt of theft of intellectual property coupled with payment of damages to the tune of one hundred million dollars has caused the FBI, Australian Police and others to claim extortion. As far as I know, they have not yet instituted lawsuits."

"I insisted in meeting the culprits face-to-face to disabuse them of any hope of succeeding in their crazy plan. In retrospect, that may not have been a wise move. Our meeting only lasted a few minutes when the Professor, after hurling abuse at me, butted me with his formidable horns and sent me flying to the floor. I grabbed his horns but was parted from him by several members of both teams. Mr. Wolford and Mr. Meerkat were both there. After we were separated, we elected to call the meeting to a close with the Muskox shouting threats as we departed. That was the last time any of us saw him."

"On our way down to the RenCen garage, we received word that there was a heavy snowfall in Cincinnati with advice that we should hold off our return trip to the next morning. Inspector Coyote can testify to the Cincinnati weather that evening."

The coyote agreed.

"So, we got rooms at the Marriott and had dinner and drinks from six until eight. I returned to my room and slept until early the next morning when we got clearance for the helicopter to head back home. It was only after we returned to Cincinnati that I heard of the Professor's demise."

"Who was with you during the evening?"

"Let's see. Mr. Wolverine; my two security chiefs and helicopter pilots, Frau Ilse Schuylkill and Colonel Wyatt Where; Mr. Meerkat; Chief Inspector Bruce Wallaroo of the Australian National Police; and Otto Otter, my Operations Manager. During the meeting, Special Agent Honey Badger had joined us via Skype."

"Have you ever been in the offices of Muskoxen Atomic Propulsion Systems Ltd.?"

"No, I have not. Wolford, have any of our staff been there?"

"No!"

"Was this your first direct encounter with the Professor?"

"He threatened litigation over a variety of trumped up complaints in the past, but I have never met him in person. Same for the Phox firm."

"I assume you didn't like him."

"Me and the rest of the world. I think you will be hard-pressed to find a friend of his, except perhaps at the law firm. I'm not even sure of them."

"So, from the time you left the meeting until you went to bed, you were in the company of some or all of your companions."

"Not entirely. After we first checked in at the hotel, I went up to my suite. I stayed there until it was time to go to dinner. A little more than an hour."

"Did you kill the Professor?"

"Absolutely not."

"How about a member of your staff?"

"Not at all likely but you'll have to ask them. Wolford? Maury?"

Two negative shakes of the head.

"Did you get that, Sergeant Racoon?"

"No sir. Will you both please state your name and answer the question."

"Wolford Wolverine. I did not kill Professor Ovibos."

"Maury Meerkat. I deny killing Professor Ovibos."

"Inspector Coyote. Can you get a statement from the rest of the party while you are there and forward it to us?"

The Cincinnati Policeman agreed.

"OK, as far as I'm concerned that wraps up this session, but your status hasn't changed, Doctor Bear. We are still very interested in you. Please turn your passport over to Inspector Coyote and keep us informed of any travel plans."

Wolford protested the taking of the passport. "You are not on very solid ground taking Doctor Bear's documents. He is hardly a flight risk and you know it. He has a high-ranking member of the Australian police with him and the FBI are also in contact with him."

"All right, Counsellor. He can keep his passport, but I want to know where he is at all times." He signed off.

I turned to Inspector Coyote and said, "A couple of members of our Detroit meeting team are not here right now. Colonel Where, Inspector Wallaroo and Otto Otter are out in the field at the moment. When they return, I'll have them pay Cincinnati PD a visit and you can get their formal denials. If you want, I can bring in Frau Ilse Schuylkill to give you a statement right now.

"Fine! Let's get this over with as soon as we can. I'm only doing this to maintain good relations with Detroit."

I called in the Frau, explained what Captain Ford wanted and asked her to answer the question "Did you kill him?" so Inspector Coyote can pass it on up to him."

The Frau marched in, bowed to the policeman and said, "Did I kill him? No! Although I suspect there are a number of animals who would have liked to. Is that all?"

Thus ended, for the moment, the interrogation of the Great Bear and Company.

Chapter Seven

The grey Wolf is from Europe, they say
And the red ones are from USA.
But no matter which kind,
You should keep this in mind.
Stay away when you hear a wolf bay!

Aboard the Ursa Minor. The Colonel was at the controls. The helicopter only requires one pilot and Bruce Wallaroo offered to fly it. Everyone was familiar with his aerobatics and he wasn't going to get the chance to try it in this ship. The Colonel gently but firmly told him he needed to be checked out and now wasn't the time. Ever seen a marsupial pout? He sat in the co-pilot seat fidgeting.

Back in the passenger compartment, Otto and Chita were getting reacquainted. At one time or another, each had saved the other's life. They both recalled their wild and near fatal adventures involving the late and unlamented criminal genius Imperius Drake. Imperius was trying to create an army of super beings in an effort to conquer the world *(or the cosmos.)* Otto was to become his experimental animal. Fortunately, the plan failed but not before seriously altering the Otter's physical and psychological makeup.

Otto was telling Chita that he seemed to be retaining his ability to zap unseen from location to location without any of the nasty side effects Imperius' genetic experiments had originally created. He had been treated and given a clean bill of health by the UUI physicians and scientists. He was also given a starring role in the Bearoness' Aquacade Revue -*Some Like It Cold*- billed as Otto the Magnificent using his "Now you see me, now you don't" talents to amuse and amaze the audience. Teleporting past locked doors; up and down elevator shafts; and through blocked passageways; he used those same gifts in helping to solve previous cases for Octavius. A surge of adrenalin seemed to trigger his abilities. Let's hope he can do it again.

Chita *(aka Madame Catherine Catt),* against her better judgment, became Imperius Drake's executive officer in a variety of schemes to separate the rich and famous from their wealth. When Imperius plotted to kill off most of the world's geneticists, as well as Octavius and the Bearoness, Chita quit. Financial chicanery? OK! Mass murder? No way! She and Imperius became mortal enemies with both trying to kill the other off. She finally succeeded, in an act of self-defense in the tunnels of an Egyptian tomb. *(See Book Five -The Curse of the Mummy's Case.)* Since that time, she has gone on to become editor-chief and publisher of several media outlets for females. She also owns a North Sea oil well and has taken on minor partnership positions with Bearoness Belinda in several of her business ventures. In spite of her spotted past, she is well liked by the Great Bear's team with one major exception – The Great Bear, himself. *(At least, that's what he says.)*

But now, both of these worthies are engaging themselves in trying to track down the Professor's killer(s) while putting the Phox Law Firm out of business permanently.

Finally convinced he was not going to fly the Ursa Minor, Chief Inspector Wallaroo bounced into the cabin and in his almost unintelligible Strine accent queried, "So what's our plan?"

Chita, flashing her diamond collar, said, "I'm going to try and involve the law firm in a case of fraud and hopefully get one or more of them disbarred. With the death of the Professor, their attempts at extortion died too. How they

68

could have come up with that unbelievable scenario is beyond me. I wonder if the Muskox had something on the partners reaching back to one of their earlier capers and forced them into cooking up that crazy scheme."

"It wasn't that crazy," said Bruce. "One of our techie firms in Australia was considering meeting part of their demands."

Otto sat up, pop-eyed. "You've got to be kidding. With his death, does MAPS Ltd. still exist? Did he have partners? How about next of kin? Can somebody still profit from this?"

"Not sure! I wouldn't be surprised if some of the law firm partners had a piece of the action. Something we need to find out."

"Anyway," said the Cat, "I have a five o'clock appointment with Phileas Phox, the firm's managing partner. What are you going to do, Brucie?"

"I'm getting together with FBI Special Agent Honey Badger to compare notes and see if we can take the Detroit PD's pressure off Octavius."

Otto said he was going to start searching the MAPS Ltd. offices assuming no one was there and then go on to the Phox firm. Entering without breaking! "I hope they don't work late. The Colonel will be working with me."

Speaking of whom, a low-pitched growl announced an upcoming arrival at DTW.

On the ground and on the way. First stop 477 Michigan Avenue and the FBI. Chief Inspector Wallaroo is meeting Special Agent Honey Badger.

"G'day, Agent Badger. Good to see you again."

"Hello, Inspector. This is a sorry mess."

"That's a fair dinkum call. Ocko has only himself to blame for this fiasco, although I'm not about to tell him that. He really wanted to face down that Muskox. They both have tempers. In the case of the Professor, "had" is the correct word. Oh, I have something for you. Do you know Senhor L. Condor?"

"Isn't he the bird who put Pontius Puma's network in the tank?"

"Right in one! Well, don't ask me how he did it, but he got a copy of the original tape of that crazy meeting and the version the Phoxes sent to the Detroit police. They don't match. Most of the Professor's rants have been erased including his attack on Ocko. The Bear comes out being the aggressor in spades. Here's the before and after versions."

"Thanks. I won't ask how the Condor got these, but I can guess. Captain Ford needs to see these. You know, I have an itch that the altercation between the Bear and the Muskox may have had nothing to do with the killing. I think the lawyers are trying to frame Octavius. He's a threat."

"Same thought crossed my mind. Do you think the lawyers killed the Muskox? If so, why?"

"He may have become too much of a liability. We two members of law enforcement need to have a chat with the Detroit Constabulary. Hold on and I'll see if he's available."

"Hello, this is Special Agent Honey Badger of the FBI here in Detroit. I'd like to speak with Captain Ford, please. Thanks! I'll hold on."

The hyper-mobile Wallaroo was having trouble restraining himself from jumping around the room. The office chair he was sitting on rolled out from under him and he ended up smashing into the Agent's desk just as the Policeman came on the line.

"Hello, Ford here! Agent Badger? What was that crash?"

"That, Captain, was Inspector Bruce Wallaroo from Australia. He slipped getting up out of his chair. We have some information relative to the

Muskox case that you ought to have. Any chance you can join us here at FBI Headquarters?"

"How about in half an hour?"

"Good, see you then."

Chapter Eight

In low light and not making a sound,
Our two heroes are looking around
In the office of MAPS
For their e-mails and Apps.
Some strange traffic is just what they found.

While the cogs of law enforcement began to mesh, Chita, Otto and the Colonel drove on to the Renaissance Center. They had all agreed to meet for dinner at 8 o'clock and then fly back to the Bear's Lair. Chita was early for her 5 o'clock appointment with Phileas Phox but Otto and the Colonel were hoping the offices of MAPS Ltd. had been deserted They climbed aboard an elevator heading for Floor 26 of 200 RenCen and arrived at a standard office building corridor. Several small enterprises - an advertising firm; two software development shops; and there at the end, a non-descript glass door with MAPS Ltd. in stationery store gold letters. No lights.

Otto looked at the Colonel. "Well here goes! Assuming nobody's there, I'll check for alarms and then let you in." He chuckled. "We don't want a suspicious looking wolf wandering around in the corridor." With that he disappeared. The Colonel could see a flashlight moving around behind the door. Then, some fiddling with the door lock and Otto standing there shooing the Colonel inside.

"For an outfit that supposedly deals in secret information and intellectual property, their physical security stinks. Come on in. I don't want to flash this light around. There's an open space with several desks and two individual offices. If the researchers had laptop computers, they took them with them. There is a desktop system in one office. I assume it belonged to the Professor. I don't want to take it. Believe it or not, the password is under the keyboard. I brought along a couple of thumb drives to offload the hard disk. That's going to take some time."

"OK," said the Colonel, "while you're doing that I'll go through any paper files they have. I wonder why the Police didn't declare this site as a crime scene. Nothing seems to have been touched. They may not believe he was murdered here."

"But wouldn't they still have wanted to do what we're doing?"

"They may already have what they think is important."

The Colonel started looking through the file drawers. Mostly incoming correspondence. One desk had paid receipts and bills. Probably the Office Manager's. A full shredder sat against the wall. It looked like most of the threatening letters originated with the law firm instead of MAPS. Although, the Professor should have had copies along with any responses.

"Not much of the paper variety. Have you copied the e-mail files?"

"Yeah and they're not encrypted. I think we may want to talk with Howard when we get back. There's a lot of traffic here with Covington Cougar. Isn't he the venture capitalist who is in Howard's confidential Group of Seven?"

"The name rings a bell. Are any of the others on this Contact list?

"Not that I've seen but I'm just skimming. I want to give this entire set of files to L. Condor when we return. He can turn them inside out."

"Otto, how much longer do you need with that computer? I think we may be overstaying our welcome here."

"You're probably right. Tell you what, Wyatt. If anyone comes, I can zap, and you can't. Although that hyperspeed thing you and the Frau do is pretty impressive. Why don't you leave now? I'll be finished in a few minutes. I'll meet you in the lobby bar at the Marriott. Order me a kelp juice and vodka. Bruce will want beer when he shows up and the Cat is on a strict Champagne diet. Don't order anything for her. She's very picky about what she drinks."

"All right. It's after five. I wonder how Chita is doing."

Chita

Chapter Nine

Spotted Chita's breathtakingly swift.
It's a really remarkable gift.
From zero to fifty
In no time. How nifty!
And just think! Not one gear must she shift!

"Good evening Mr. Phox. It's kind of you to see me on such short notice."

"Our pleasure, Madame Catt. How can we be of service?" The Weasel had taken his eyes from the Cheetah's long legs to the magnificent diamond choker that circled her spotted neck. This could be an interesting and profitable case.

"I only plan to be in Detroit for a few days. My home is in London, England. I'm afraid I'm in a rather delicate situation. This necklace you see was given to me by a very good friend here in Motor City. I should say a 'former' good friend. He is in the entertainment industry. Well, it turns out that it really wasn't his to give and the previous owner wants it back. I am highly reluctant to give it up. Let's just say I have become attached to it. I have been told that your firm is quite skilled in dealing with irregular affairs and to be perfectly blunt, I am looking for a way to establish my ownership of this lovely piece of jewelry. On my return to England, I probably will have to declare it and I have no documentation to support my title. Is that something you might be able to help me with. I'd be ever so grateful."

The lawyer wasn't born yesterday, and his suspicions were aroused but what the hell, greed took over. Let's see how grateful she could be. "Well,

Madame, this is a bit outside our normal practices and while we two are being perfectly blunt, it borders on the illegal. Notice please that I said 'borders.' It sounds like you and this good friend have come to a parting of the ways."

"Indeed we have. He's going to have to explain his way out of this with his former girlfriend. I'm sure he can afford to replace the necklace if she insists. But I have possession of this one and I am in no mood to give it up. But I do need to be able to prove ownership. I'm not going to involve him. That could turn into a nasty and possibly public row. I have a reputation in England to uphold. No, what I want is credible and foolproof evidence that the necklace belongs to me. Do you have connections in the jewelry business? I have had several bad experiences in the past working with dealers directly."

"They can be a rather sharp bunch. However, I think I may be able to find an established jeweler who would be willing to write you a bill of sale that would stand up to scrutiny. You will have to pay him for the service and we will expect recompense for acting as your agent."

"I suspected as much. How much will that cost?"

"I'm not sure of the jeweler but our usual fee is 10% of the value of the transaction. Now, if you will leave the necklace with me, I will personally take on the assignment." *(Without telling his partners.)*

"After all the nonsense I've been through with this bauble, I'm reluctant to let go of it. Why don't we set up a meeting with this jeweler where he or she can examine the diamonds in your and my presence and we can come to terms. It will have to be in the next few days. Otherwise, I may be forced to engage in a little smuggling."

The weasel laughed, "Oh, we wouldn't want you to do that. Please call me tomorrow about noon. I will probably have made arrangements by then."

The cat stared at him briefly, stood and rising to her full height, said, "Oh, thank you. I can see that my contact was right about your firm."

"Who is that?"

"Oh, that would be telling. See you tomorrow??"

She strode, as only Chita can stride, out of the office leaving Phileas Phox shaking his head and mentally counting his upcoming commission.

Down in the Marriott lobby bar, she met the Colonel. "How did it go?" they both asked and fell into a fit of laughter. Chita ordered a bowl of Champagne: Bearier-Jouet.

The Wolf went first. "Otto is just wrapping up downloading data from the Professor's desktop computer. The office was closed so we had free access to the files and the Muskox' e-mail. Their security is atrocious. Surprisingly, the Police haven't secured the place and I'm not sure any of the staff is still employed there. Anyway, it seems one of Howard's special colleagues was keeping up a busy correspondence with the Professor. The venture capitalist, Covington Cougar. Otto has it all on several thumb drives. Speaking of whom. Here's Otto. Bartender! One kelp juice and vodka!" They both looked at the Otter and asked, "How did it go?" evoking another round of laughter. Otto stared at them. "No problem snatching the data. Now we need L. Condor to sort it all out. What happened with you , Chita?"

"Well, I got old Phileas to agree to act as my agent in producing a fraudulent bill of sale for my diamond necklace. I told him I wanted to use it to fool British Customs. The ironic part is, the necklace is actually mine and I do have a legitimate bill of sale. Not sure it's enough to hang him out to dry but I doubt the local Bar Association will be pleased. It's probably entrapment, so I doubt we can trigger criminal proceedings. He is undoubtedly doing it without his partners' knowledge. I'm sure they would have wanted a piece of the action even if it was only a few thousand dollars."

"Are you actually going through with the transaction? Where does that put you?"

"There's no way I'm going to go any further with this charade, but I do have our entire interview recorded. I have a wire and microchip tucked into my choker. He wanted me to leave the necklace with him, so he could show it to a shady jeweler. File that under Fat Chance! I probably would never have seen it again. No, he's expecting me to call him tomorrow. He won't like what he hears. We'll have to talk to Wolford and Bruce about next steps, if any. I just want to make him nervous and discourage any more extortion activity on his part."

Otto slurped his vodka, "Are there still people in the Phox offices? I'd like to do a quick in and out. Think it's worth it?"

"I don't know! I met Phileas in a small office by the reception area. Clearly not his. I don't think he wanted anyone else to know about our meeting. The receptionist had left by the time our session was over, but I suspect there were still some folks at their desks. Law firms have no strict working hours. What do you want to peek at?"

"I'd like to look at the partners' computers, but they're probably password protected. Probably it's better to have Condo or Ursula hack into them. Any news from Bruce and the Badger?"

"Last I heard from Bruce, they had invited the Detroit policeman to join them at FBI Headquarters. They wanted to pass on a copy of the original tape that the Condor had downloaded. The police already have the altered version from the law firm."

Chapter Ten

Honey Badgers are fierce as can be.
They'll arrest anyone they can see.
Whether criminal rats,
Or felonious cats.
I don't think I'd like one chasing me.

The FBI Forensics Lab had just delivered several copies of each tape to Agent Badger and they set them up to show to Captain Ford, when he arrived. The alterations were pretty amateurish, dropping most of the Professor's words and actions and making Octavius out to be the aggressor. Clearly, the Phox Firm had no compunction about trying to frame the Great Bear. Speaking of bears, the Grizzly knocked on the Special Agent's door and after shaking paws all around, sat down on his haunches in front of her desk."

"OK, what do you have to show me."

"First off," said Bruce, "We'd rather keep confidential how we obtained this information. If it becomes necessary to use it in pursuit of the case, we can negotiate it at that time. Now, you've seen the tape of the meeting sent to you by the law firm."

"Right! Octavius Bear comes across as the primary antagonist."

"Well" said the Badger, "we'd like to disabuse you of that opinion. Albeit, there was clearly no love lost between the two of them. Here is the original tape of the meeting."

They watched as the action unfolded, leaving no doubt that the Muskox made a violent attempt to harm Octavius.

"Well," said the Grizzly, "That puts a different spin on things, but it only adds more fuel to the fire as far as motive is concerned. The Kodiak was assaulted and fought back. After he was hustled out of the room, he may have let his temper build up even further and decided to take things into his own paws."

"OK, let's hold that thought for the moment. What I want to know is why The Phoxes created the phony version of the tape. We believe they were trying to frame Octavius and shift the blame away from the true killer."

"So, you think one or more of the lawyers is the killer?'

"We're not sure but it certainly raises a cloud of suspicion. By the way, has the coroner come up with a time of death?"

"He's still working on it. The Muskox was already dead when he was dumped in the river. He did not drown."

"That sets off a number of questions. Where and when was he killed? By whom? It would have taken a lot of strength to kill him off and then use some kind of carrier to transport his body from his office to the river. It would be damned difficult to make that trip without someone noticing. So far, no one has reported seeing anything like that. We've been making inquiries all along the Winter Garden and riverside."

"Maybe he wasn't dead yet. More likely, he went to the river on his own power and was fatally attacked there by person or persons unknown. His body was found floating near the cruise ship dock."

"Why would he go to the river?"

"To meet his killer. A secret get together? There was no sign of a struggle in his office. According to his secretary/office manager, he was alive

81

and in a terrible mood when they closed down for the night. He stayed on alone, but we don't know for how long."

"I can't imagine him meeting with Octavius."

"Probably not, but at this stage, we can't discount any possibility."

"Well, where do we go from here?"

"For openers," said Captain Ford, "I want answers from the law firm about the major discrepancies in these two tapes. Fabricating false evidence in a murder investigation can be a felony and those guys know it. I want the identity of the culprit or culprits and I want to know if it was done with the partners' knowledge. That would make them co-conspirators. Meanwhile, Octavius is still an 'Animal of Interest.' Thanks for your help."

"Inspector Wallaroo, you have no official standing in this case, but I welcome your assistance. You have enough history with US criminal procedure to know when you're crossing a line. For the time being, I'll look the other way on how the original tape was discovered."

"Agent Badger, please keep in touch. I'll let you know the coroner's report. What you do with it is your business."

After he left, Bruce looked at Honey Badger and said, "I guess we couldn't have expected much more. There's more to this than a spontaneous free-for-all between the Professor and Ocko. The idea that the Muskox was meeting his future killer at the riverside has set my nose to tickling."

"Me, too. I think the Professor had another set of irons on the fire and it did him in. I guess your crew is heading back to Cincinnati. Let's set up a conference call tomorrow after you've all had a chance to digest and cross pollinate."

"Speaking of digestion, do you want to join us for dinner?

"Thanks, but I think there are things you're going to discuss that I don't want to know about. Talk to you tomorrow."

Chapter Eleven

The Antilōpine Wallaroo
Is a Wallaby plus Kangaroo.
His large feet - (macropod!)
Make him look rather odd
But I bet he moves faster than you.

After they all regrouped in the Marriott lobby bar, the consensus was for a quick round of snacks and then back to the Ursa Minor. It was about 8:30 when they descended on the DTW General Aviation Terminal and the helicopter. The Colonel had left instructions for refueling and he gave the chopper a thorough going over before letting the rest of them board. Registering with Air Traffic Control and the local tower, he got a 9:15 departure slot. The Ursa Minor had the latest and most comprehensive instrumentation for night flying and the Colonel was fully checked out on it.

This provided Chita with some relief. In the best of circumstances, she was nervous about whirlybirds, especially the variety that service her North Sea oil rig. Her buddy Otto did his best to distract her, first with a rundown on his exploration of the MAPS Ltd. e-mail system and then with stories of his latest routines with the Aquabears back at the Bearoness' Polar Paradise. They also briefly reminisced about their misadventures with Imperius Drake.

Then Chita entertained with her interview with Phileas Phox. She showed off her necklace-based recording system, courtesy of UUI's techie geniuses. They both agreed that Phileas was truly a weasel.

Still not allowed near the controls, Inspector Wallaroo had to content himself with sitting *(actually, bouncing up and down)* in the co-pilot seat up in the cockpit. Octavius would have had a major ursine eruption if he thought for one moment that Bruce was in charge of his aeronautical wonder.

Ninety minutes later, as they touched down at the Bear's Lair heliport, the Bearoness and Octavius stood off to the side waiting for them. The Bearoness had allowed the Cubs to stay up, much to the chagrin of Mlle Woof who was convinced they would never get to sleep after the big arrival. She was probably right. True to form, they capered around the platform, coming too close for comfort to the whirling blades. Hearing that the travelers had only ingested some snacks, the Frau was busy in the kitchen whipping up something more substantial. And I resumed my role as your humble narrator.

"There they are, Uncle Maury! There they are!" Amid the juvenile outbursts, L. Condor, Ursula and Howard joined the reception committee, each waiting to start their respective tasks. Marlin, as usual, was hooked up from his tank. As soon as the ship settled in, the Flying Tigers emerged to take charge of the post flight activities. In short, "Hail, Hail! the Gangs All Here!"

Otto and Chita were first out followed by Bruce Wallaroo. The Colonel stayed on to work with the Tigers.

"Well," said Octavius, "what do we know now that we didn't know before?"

Otto handed over his thumb drives to L. Condor. "Here's the Professor's e-mail. It's going to need some analysis and correlation." He turned to Howard, "I think you have a problem with one of your Confidential Seven. Covington Cougar seems to have been a very active communicator with the Professor. I haven't had a chance to research it and I hope L. Condor can, but it seems the two of them were engaged in a dialogue on your activities. We'll get you the specifics."

Needless to say, Howard was not pleased.

Inspector Wallaroo looked over at Octavius. "Ocko, sorry to say, you are still an 'Animal of Interest' for the Detroit Police Department but given the difference in the two tapes, they are becoming much more inclined to the theory that you are being set up by the law firm. I trust Captain Ford to be fair and objective. Remember, nobody up there is enamored of the Phoxes. The FBI seems to be on your side. We made some progress. The best current theory is that the Professor met his killer at the riverside for unknown reasons, was dispatched there and tossed overboard."

"The Muskox did not drown, and it's not likely he was killed elsewhere and transported to the river. If that was the case, the murderer could have dumped the body anywhere. The riverside was probably a convenient location for a face-to-face meeting. What the meeting was all about and who was involved besides the Professor is still a mystery. But that animal could have been anyone armed with a hefty weapon. That means it may not have taken a large, strong animal such as yourself to do him in. However, it may have been an effort to push him in the water. Small steps but in the right direction."

Chita told her story about Phileas the Phoxy Weasel. She was waiting until tomorrow to tell him he had been set up by her to facilitate a case of customs fraud. Her recording was being sent to the Phox partners, the State Bar of Michigan, the Police and the FBI. Just another shot across the bow, so to speak. Everything we can do to keep Phileas cross footed is a help.

Octavius thanked the team, turned to Belinda and said, "Let's get the twins to bed and maybe a little mead might be in order."

L. Condor took the thumb drives from Otto and headed to his lab. No doubt he would spend the night with Ursula untangling the Professor's e-mails, establishing incoming and outgoing patterns and sorting out relationships.

Howard and Marlin took up the correspondence and history of their Confidential Seven. Was there anything in the Professor's e-mails that dealt with alternate universes? They'd soon see. The Multiverse Electron Pairing project has so far been a one-way trip. Several experiments have succeeded in coupling electrons in our universe with ones in an alternate planet. But no successful attempt had yet been made to set up a pairing that originates from another world. Soon! Soon! Watch this *(outer)* space.

The Colonel has had the most involvement in multiverse travel starting with experiments in the military and proceeding further under Octavius' sponsorship. In Canada *(Book 4 The Lower Case)* the team encountered several denizens of an alternative world. In Egypt *(Book 5 The Curse of the Mummy's Case)* they had established that the ancient Underworlds to which dead souls were transported had all the characteristics of multiverse domains. Other terrestrials were reporting similar experiences. Four of Howard's Confidential Seven had deep expertise either in quantum physics or alternate universe studies. Howard and Marlin seemed to be the sole members of the group who played in both ballparks. Covington Cougar was primarily a project facilitator. As soon as L. Condor and Ursula sorted through the electronic tangles, Howard would be contacting each participant individually.

I wandered into Condo's lab to check their progress just in time to hear my own voice say, "I think that should wrap it up. Oh, Hello Maury."

Octavius responded, "Wonderful job, Senhor Condor!" followed by a giggle.

"Are you two playing speech games again?"

"Of course," said the Condor in his baseline normal voice, "It keeps us from getting bored. We haven't figured out yet how many variations we can produce but it must be in the thousands."

"Millions!" said the AI's soft, usual vocal sound.

"Showoffs!" I retorted to two peals of laughter.

Chapter Twelve

Sci-Fi stories have ferrets galore.
Antique paintings and statues show more.
In the future and past
Their appeal is quite vast.
In the present, They're simply a bore.

Little did Phileas Phox know how much trouble was going rain down on him and his cohorts that morning. The opening salvo was fired by a Detroit PD-FBI combo. Captain Ford invited the senior partners to his office with a strong suggestion that failure to appear would not bode well. Felicity, the Ferret, wanted to push back and not show up but cooler heads prevailed. *(the weasel, Phileas Phox and the skunk, Farrington Foxx.)*

"We need to find out what this is all about," said the skunk, his first contribution to the dialogue. At 10 AM, the three partners marched into the Police conference room, nodded to the Badger and staring at the Grizzly, Phileas asked, "What is this all about?"

"Fabricated evidence, which in the case of a murder can amount to a felony. You guys are too cute for your own good. Here is the meeting tape you sent us which strongly implies that Dr. Octavius Bear had motive, means and opportunity for killing the Professor. I suggest you watch and listen carefully."

He ran the heavily edited tape. "Is that the recording you gave us?"

The skunk nodded. The weasel and ferret remained silent. "Now, let me run the original version that came from your files. Don't bother protesting about how we got it. We got it. You'll notice the Muskox' attack on the Kodiak; the bear defending himself; the abusive language of the Professor and

89

the need for him to be restrained. All of that and more was deleted from this original when you submitted the copy to us. You couldn't leave well enough alone. The forensics labs of the FBI and our own department detected the rather clumsy editing. Whoever did it was a rank amateur."

The skunk looked around anywhere but at the policeman or special agent.

"Now, I wouldn't want to accuse three members of the legal community of trying to frame an 'Animal of Interest' but you can see how we might come to that conclusion. Counsellors, your credibility is shot. We cannot use any of the so-called evidence you have provided. Dr. Bear's lawyer is aware of the alterations and is prepared to sue your firm and each of you individually. We haven't decided whether to file criminal charges or not. How you react will have a strong bearing on what we do."

The ever-aggressive Felicity hissed. "You break into our files and consider filing charges against us? We'll sue you both and your departments."

The weasel glared at the ferret and said, "Shut up, Felicity. We don't need that kind of problem. All right, Captain. We'll withdraw the tape and any other material we sent you. We still believe Octavius Bear is the killer, but we'll leave that for you to determine. We'll contact Mr. Wolverine and try to avert any law suits he plans to bring forth."

Special Agent Badger stared at him in disbelief. "You don't get off that easy, Phileas. There is the small matter of the threatened extortion you have been carrying out on behalf of your now deceased client. Your letters need to be recalled and all efforts in that regard immediately brought to a close. We'll want proof that you have rescinded your worldwide pressures and intimidations. That was a dumb stunt in the first place. The State Bar of

Michigan is aware of your activities. What they plan to do is up to them. You might want to consider an alternate career."

The Phox Partners rose and proceeded out of police headquarters. Phileas and Felicity turned on the skunk. "When you said the altered tape would be an airtight indictment of Octavius Bear, we believed you. Instead, your ineptitude has dumped us on the road to disbarment. If you didn't know how to handle the technology, why didn't you use someone who did?"

"Now wait a minute! It was you who wanted to keep knowledge of this set up to the fewest possible number of participants. You both know we don't trust most of our associates and staff."

The ferret hissed once again. "I swear, Farrington, I don't know how you made partner. How can we possibly trust you to keep us from being hung out to dry? You're an idiot."

When they arrived back at their offices, there was a message waiting for Phileas. Madame Catt had called. She was not going to meet with him, but she wanted him to hear a recording which she had sent to his partners, the Detroit PD, the State Bar and the FBI. He listened to his own voice promising to set up a meeting with a dishonest jeweler who was willing to provide, for a significant fee, a fraudulent certified sales certificate for her diamond necklace. It would certainly stand up to British Customs scrutiny. He also heard himself telling her that the firm's fee for such a transaction was ten percent of the jeweler's charge.

Thunderstruck, he hung up the phone just in time for Felicity to come storming into his office. "I am surrounded by cretins. Isn't it bad enough we got caught with our phony tape? Now, you have to get us set up with an entrapment situation. Cheating your partners is the crowning blow. I want you and Farrington to resign effectively immediately. It's the only way we can save the firm, if you even care."

"Now Felicity!"

"Don't you 'now Felicity' me. I'm the only competent member of management left, and I swear I'll go to the State Bar myself and see that the two of you go down in flames."

And so, as we temporarily bid farewell to the rapidly disintegrating Phox Law Firm, we turn our attention back to the yet unsolved murder of Professor Hercules Ovibos.

Chapter Thirteen

Is he mountain lion, cougar or puma(r)?

Is he nasty or is that a rumor?

For he has this distinction.

He is facing extinction.

That can impact a cat's sense of humor.

Condo had spent the night along with Ursula sorting through the Professor's e-mails and confirmed Otto's suppositions. One name kept showing up: Covington Cougar – Venture Capitalist with Space Enterprises LLC. Howard was not pleased, especially when it became clear that they could now almost create electron linkage from another world. They were nearing success. Professor Karl Shepherd of MIT and Doctor Susanna Shrike of Cal Tech were conducting experiments to confirm Howard's and Marlin's design.

The Cougar was passing on the team's progress reports to the Muskox who in turn was publishing the work as his own. He then developed the idea of suing any and all organizations that were pursuing or thinking about pursuing work related to electron coupling. It only took a short elevator ride to the Phox firm to convince them that there was money to be made supporting the Professor's crazy scheme. Greed conquered all until the Muskox ended up floating in the Detroit River.

When Marlin heard Condo's news, after several flips in his tank, he said to Howard. "OK, whom do we trust? Ursula, were any of the other team members on the Professor's e-mail?"

A soft, sultry, female voice responded. "No, Marlin. Just the Cougar."

"Do we approach our other colleagues and tell them about the Cougar's betrayal?"

Howard replied "I think we have to. We don't want them innocently feeding Covington with more information."

"But with the Muskox dead, what's he going to do with the data?"

Ursula replied. "My research says there are plenty of other parties who might be interested. The Professor may not have been the only beneficiary of the Cougar's slippery data transfers."

Howard sulked, "For all we know, the whole project may be blown. So much for limiting the team. Can you imagine if General Turmoil got his hooves on our data?"

(General Turmoil is a Horse who heads up a Federal Government sponsored, semi-military, semi-spy organization called The Business. He has been actively pursuing alternative universes with conquest in mind. Octavius has been at odds with him for a long time and Colonel Where, while he was still in the Army, ended up as an experimental subject of the General's. All told, a nasty equine piece of work.)

"Yes, I can, and I don't like it one bit.

"All right! First stops: Karl Shepherd and Susanna Shrike. We need to tell them their experiments were probably compromised by the Cougar."

They decided to use encrypted phones. No e-mail message trail, although the conversations could be recorded. They reached Karl and gave him the bad news. First reaction: String up Covington Cougar but only after recovering the data he stole and passed on. Second reaction: Change passwords and crypto algorithms. Third reaction: Hack into Covington's systems and see who else has been communicating with him. Ursula was already hard at work on this last chore.

Susanna had similar suggestions although she had even fiercer thoughts on what to do with the Cougar. Tough lady, especially when her precious work was involved.

Howard and Marlin then took on the equally thankless tasks of updating Commander Cormorant and Alfred Armadillo. Had Covington contacted either of them recently? Not in the last few weeks and then it had been a joint progress report with all hands on deck. The Commander wondered where the Cougar would take his wares now that the Muskox was no more. General Turmoil was on the top of his list. But it's not the General's style to buy when he could snatch. Condo and Ursula were experiencing some difficulty hacking into the Cougar's systems. A sure sign Covington was getting some sophisticated tech support. Not enough to stop Condo but it slowed him down a bit. Could that be the none too subtle hoof of General Turmoil at work?

Just where is Covington Cougar? Did he do in the Professor? If so, why?

Time to brief The Great Bear. I found him in his office and he was awake!

First things first. "Octavius, it seems one of the Confidential Group that Howard and Marlin have been working with has been double dealing. The Professor's e-mail has been chock-full of progress reports from the scientists. The source of all this information is Covington Cougar, whose whereabouts is currently unknown. We have our suspicions but no proof that he may be the murderer. They may have had a falling out of some sort."

"We also suspect that General Turmoil may be involved with the Cougar but again, no definitive proof. The Professor may have been getting in the General's way and was eliminated."

The Great Bear snarled, "The Detroit Police and the FBI should know about this. We need to find Covington tout suite. I understand that the Cougar's treachery doesn't categorically prove he's the killer, but it should certainly get him registered as an 'Animal of Interest.' What makes you think the General may be involved?"

"Primarily, the subject matter! He has devoted so much time and effort on alternative universes and has so many resources at his disposal that it would surprise me no end if he didn't know about Howard and his cohorts. Whether he's been able to penetrate the entire group is up for grabs. But now that we know there is at least one weak link, I'm willing to bet the Horse and possibly others have been on top of our group's progress."

"Maury, I'm half tempted to shut the project down. After all, it's my money that's supporting this effort."

"Not entirely! The other members have also been using small parcels of unobtrusively sourced private funds to support some of their efforts. They wouldn't be able to go on as freely if you yanked the rug, but you are not entirely in charge. Besides, you'd be playing right into the General's hands, if he is indeed involved. Getting you out of the alternate universe entangled electron space would leave the field wide open for him. If he has much of the team's research and progress materials in his hooves, he may be well on his way to taking charge. We also don't know if any other groups are involved."

"Aren't you a ray of sunshine? OK, tell Howard his project is still a GO, but we need to get our paws around his group and upgrade personal and technical security. Meanwhile, let's see if law enforcement can get a fix on Covington Cougar. What does Bruce Wallaroo have to say about all of this?"

"Bruce has been concentrating on the Phox Law Firm but I'm not sure the lawyers even know about the Cougar. The Professor, after all, has been claiming all of the intellectual property as his own inventions, theories and research. He certainly wouldn't have admitted that it was all stolen if he was trying to make his lawsuits stick. I'm sure we haven't heard the last of the Phoxes, but we may have the delightful privilege of watching them crash and burn."

"Well, make sure Wolford keeps up the pressure on them. We can't sue the Professor, but we can make life miserable for those shysters." said the Bear. "Ask Howard to drop by my office."

Thus dismissed, I went off in search of the Porcupine. In the process, I ran into Condo.

"What's new in the world of clandestine communications?"

The Condor sighed. "No new traffic. The Cougar is obviously aware of the Muskox' demise and has stopped sending to him. In fact, he's not active at all which strikes me as passing strange."

"Got a theory?"

The Bird replied, "He's probably lying low. I'm sure, by now, he knows his identity and collusion have been blown. He's been excluded from the group's activities and any attempt to rejoin the club has been rebuffed. I know you guys think General Turmoil has a hoof in this and you may be right. I think I told you that the Cougar's links have been very strongly protected by a techie source well above his personal capability. But even those links are no longer active."

"The cops and FBI are searching for him at this moment. They have declared him an 'Animal of Interest' in the Professor's death. Any ideas where he may be?"

"Maury, Space Enterprises LLC has offices in Florida not far from the Kennedy Space Center. They have been involved in funding a number of experimental space shots with other non-governmental organizations. Covington Cougar's principal forté seems to be packaging programs and selling them to interested parties. His role with our group seems to be structuring ventures to create off-planet electron coupling. He is not a technological wizard, but he does understand the logistical and financial pluses and minuses of creating space-based projects. If he's there, he's not using their telecom facilities. I suspect he has taken a bunk."

"Do you think he may have been in Detroit when the Muskox took his swim?"

"Well, he's high on my personal list of possible Professor Pushers but I have a hard time coming up with a motive unless of course, the Muskox became too demanding or refused to live up to any financial arrangements they had made."

"That would certainly fit the Professor's Personality Profile, Condo. His popularity index was about as low as you can get and still exist."

"Which he no longer does!!"

"Too true! Oh, here comes Howard! His Bearship wants to speak with you in his office."

"Oh great! Just what I needed. This will certainly make my day."

"Actually, all things considered, he seems to be in a pretty good mood."

"Well, I'll try not to screw that up.

98

The Development of Civilization
Volume Seven - Part Three
<u>Welcome to the Sub-Atomic World</u>

(From "An Introduction to Faunapology"
by Octavius Bear Ph.D.)

Most animals have a rudimentary familiarity with Physics, the natural science that seeks to precisely define and find relationships among the most fundamental measurable quantities in the universe. It involves the study of matter and its motion and behavior through space and time, along with related concepts such as energy and force. We are pretty comfortable with those phenomena that we can see, hear, taste, touch or mentally visualize. We have an incomplete but usually sufficient understanding of electricity, magnetism, hydraulics, optics and sound, for example, to lead our lives without too much concern. It's when the dimensions of the universe expand incredibly (intergalactic space, black holes, light speed) or contract to the infinitesimal that we get nervous and often want to hide somewhere.

Let's take a moment and look at the world inside the atom, once thought to be the absolutely indivisible makeup of the universe. Turns out it's not. There's a lot going on inside the atom. That's what Particle Physics is all about. Often referred to as Quantum Physics, scientists have been exploring, quantifying and cataloguing sub-atomic components with exotic names like fermions, quarks and leptons. One form of lepton, the electron, may sound familiar because it has been used and misused in all sorts of situations.

Near the end of the twentieth century, to put a little order into this apparent chaos, scientists pulled everything they knew about Quantum Physics into one massive equation — the Standard Model of Particle Physics. It is very much a work in progress. So far, twelve basic particles have been identified but they can be combined into more complex entities. In addition to the particles, there are also four fundamental forces that propel this part of the universe: the strong force, weak force, the electromagnetic force, and gravity. Unfortunately, gravity is not a good fit for the Standard Model. The other three forces are supported by particles known as bosons. A major use of the Standard Model is not just to identify and catalog. It has a major predictive role. In 2012, the so-called Higgs boson that provides particles with mass and had been predicted by the Model was found at CERN's Large Hadron Collider. CERN is the European Organization for Nuclear Research. The Large Hadron Collider (LHC) is the world's largest and most powerful particle accelerator.

There is a massive amount of literature, some of it understandable by the average bear, dealing with Particle Physics. Recommended Reading if you are so moved!

This is all very interesting (?!) but does Particle Physics have any practical application besides keeping a lot of scientists very busy and spending a lot of money on exotic equipment? The answer is "Yes!"

Nuclear batteries; biomedicine and drug development; cancer therapy; diagnostic instruments; nuclear monitoring; turbulence analysis and prediction; enhanced power transmission; computing and telecommunications tools; cryptographic and other security technologies; super enhanced light sources, just to name a few.

As far as Particle Physics goes, the old saying applies: "Be Sure to Sweat the Small Stuff."

Chapter Fourteen

Is the Dolphin a mammal or fish?
You can choose either one as you wish.
While the mammal cavorts
In aquatic resorts,
The poor Pompano's served on a dish.

"Come on in, Howard. You too, Maury. Let me get Marlin and Ursula linked into the conversation."

L. Condor and the UUI techies had set up an in-house video and data network so the Dolphin could communicate from his outsized tank with anyone and everyone inside the mansion and labs, selected areas in UUI and any of the multiple aircraft and vehicles in use by the team. He also had access to Ursula, external Internet connections and smart phone hookups. In short, Marlin was the ultimate sharer. Given his brain power, he was a welcome participant in almost any discussion. To ensure his privacy, he controlled access to his system, but he could be overridden by Octavius and Howard. All in all, an efficient communication and research environment.

"Marlin? Octavius! Howard, Maury and Ursula are here with me and we want you to join us in discussing the events of the past few days. *(That was news to Howard.)*

A bottle-nosed face appeared on the office screen and after a few adjustments, the Dolphin's squeaky sounds converted themselves into American English courtesy of the UUI Underwater SeaPod Translator, a product of the combined genius of Howard, L. Condor, Ursula, Marlin and UUI technicians.

Originally developed for the Prince of Whales as a "Thank You" for his assistance in tracking down undersea anomalies in the North Sea *(Book Three – The Case of Scotch)* the device had become a best seller for UUI. Profits are shared with the Prince and have thus extended Marlin's stay with The Great Bear's team. His original assignment was as the Prince's Court Jester cum Technical Guru. He may have to return to the Prince's realm someday, but for the moment, he is more than earning his keep with Octavius.

"OK, let me get right to it. The short version: The work you and your confidential team have been doing has been compromised. We strongly believe Covington Cougar is the culprit and was responsible for passing data on to the Professor. The Muskox probably promised him a share of any money he extorted through his lawsuits. My personal belief is that the Cougar didn't stop there. After all, he's probably too smart to fall for the Professor's harebrained schemes but still too greedy to take a pass on even a wildly improbable opportunity to make a profit. I'll bet that's what the law firm thought as well. Even screwballs hit it right once in a while. What have we got to lose? Plenty, in the case of the Phoxes."

"But who else would have an interest in what you must admit is pretty esoteric science? Interplanetary coupling of electrons may be good for a possible Noble Prize but is there a pot of gold at the end of that particular rainbow? We're involved because of our Multiverse Project. Alternative worlds have major consequences for our civilization. We've already experienced a few. Quantum capable alternative worlds are as yet indescribable, but the implications are certainly there. So, I ask you two. Who else is in this space? *(No pun intended!)* I'll bet on General Turmoil and his underlings. Are there others? Are we the only game in town?"

Howard snuffled and then said, "L.Condor and Ursula have been busy tracking the e-mails of our group. We probably should get them in here."

"Good idea! Maury, can you get a hold of Big Bird? Call up Ursula. While you're at it, bring in the Colonel. He's been checking the scientists credentials and backgrounds."

Off I went. As I left the office, I practically fell over Condo. I tugged on his wing. "His Bearship requires your presence in our discussions. Do join us! Why should we be having all the fun?"

Calling on his embedded speech generator, *(Another UUI wonder. Condors do not have a voice box.)* he did a perfect Bugs Bunny, "Nyaah! What's up, Doc?"

"We're trying to define the wobbling electron landscape. You and Ursula have had your probes in the e-mails of Howard's team plus any other players who may be involved."

"That we have! *(Back to Condor normal)* Happy to share our ill-gotten knowledge."

Octavius shouted, "Come in, Senhor Condor, come in. We are brainstorming the situation with the science data leakage and Covington Cougar. Your brain and Ursula's are more than welcome."

"Thank you, Doctor Bear! Well, it's clear that there was substantial traffic going on between the Cougar and Muskox. Howard and Marlin will have to tell you just how much information was transferred and how valuable it was. We have created a sequential file of all the transmissions. Just about all of the messages were one-way – Cougar to Muskox with only acknowledgements of receipt from the Professor. The encryption used was fairly sophisticated and we believe, beyond the inventive skill of either of the parties. Some other technical support was at work. I'm not going to guess who that might be but since you seem to think General Turmoil and The Business might be involved, let me say that this is well within their capability. Oddly enough, there is no evidence of any interchanges by the Cougar and The Business."

Ursula added, "There are a series of rather innocuous network maintenance documents sent out to the Cloud that may hide encoded material. It would call for state-of-the-art techniques but well within the realm of possibility. I haven't tried to analyze any of them, but I will, if you wish."

"Please do, if you can spare the time."

"Of course. Those cloud-based documents could be available to anyone who had the proper credentials."

"In other words, accessible to the highest bidder or bidders armed with the technology?"

"But remember, I doubt the Cougar could handle the technology by himself."

Octavius turned to Howard and Marlin's image. "Do we have any inkling as to where the Cougar is?"

Marlin responded, "He's been quiet for almost twenty-four hours. Condo has been monitoring his Florida facilities."

The Bird intervened, "I suspect that once he realized he was being shut out by the rest of the team, Covington decided to go silent."

The Colonel joined us. "Or," said he. "he has been silenced."

Speaking of silence, that's what the Wolf's remark evoked.

"Well," the Bear finally replied, "there's an interesting prospect. OK, you two, just what the hell has your group been uncovering that could cost the life of one, possibly two involved individuals. Let us suppose that the Professor's death had nothing to do with the lawsuits but instead was tied to the information he possessed courtesy of the Cougar. I doubt if the Muskox cared what the information really meant as long as he could use it for his extortion plans. Let us further suppose that the Cougar had no realization of the true value and impact of the stuff he was feeding the Muskox. After all, of the team, he had the least scientific credentials. He was on board primarily for packaging and promoting the work you guys are developing. Am I right?"

Howard and Marlin both agreed.

"Then, may I suggest that we embark on a very careful analysis of who your team is and what they have uncovered on the assumption that a knowledgeable third party already knows the implications of your discoveries and may find it worth killing for."

Howard jumped in. "Whoa, Octavius, you are leaping to a lot of unsupported conclusions here. First, we don't know whether the Professor's death was tied to the information he had. Two, we don't know if anything has happened to Covington Cougar. Three, we don't know what the Cougar had in mind providing the Professor with the data. Four, we don't know if a knowledgeable third party really exists although there is some evidence to support that theory. I want to scrub those e-mails that Condo captured and see what, if anything shapes up."

"Sounds like a good plan to me, Howard, but first let's talk about the team. Then, have at the e-mails. How much time do you and Marlin need? You're not the 'Animal of Interest' here in the death of the Professor. I am. In addition to getting to the bottom of this whole mess, I want to get my name completely cleared ASAP."

"Give us twenty-four hours. We could use some help here, Condo. You too, Ursula."

"Delighted to assist."

"OK," said The Bear, "but first let's do a little vetting of your scientific compadres. First on the list. Professor Karl Shepherd Ph.D.-MIT Quantum Mechanics Laboratory. What's his background and why did you team up with him?"

The Colonel intervened. "Octavius, I've been checking credentials on all of this team. If there is a 'Who's Who in Quantum Physics,' Karl Shepherd will lead the list. His curriculum vitae goes on for pages; he has pulled down just about all the relevant awards except the Noble Prize. He is affiliated with most, if not all, of the Quantum Mechanics societies and research organizations; has authored several books and God knows, how many papers. He has worked with the US government on several major projects and still carries a teaching load at MIT."

Howard looked over and said, "Thanks, Wyatt. The real question is: 'Why did he team up with us?' The Alternate Universe aspect of our work is what captured his attention. He is a disciplined manager of experimental processes and he and Susanna Shrike have been taking our theories and putting them into meaningful practice."

Octavius let out one of his characteristic "Hmmms" and said to Howard. "Let me ask you this. Do you think he's a killer?"

We were all dumbstruck at the question.

Howard gulped and asked, "Are you serious?"

The Great Bear snorted, "Need I remind you that I am currently regarded as an 'Animal of Interest' in the Professor's death. Is it any more likely that I killed him than Doctor Shepherd? We have to take every possibility into consideration, no matter how improbable it might seem. Now what about Dr. Shrike? You characterized her as a tough bird. She comes from a long line of bloody killers, but I doubt she's big enough to take on a Muskox by herself. Just what are Extraterrestrial Studies as practiced at Caltech?"

Ursula responded, "Just what the name suggests. The study of other worlds. She came to us as a result of one of her colleagues mentioning Project Multiverse. Alternate biospheres and ecospheres are right up her alley. She's brilliant, opinionated and very frequently correct, but she can also be very nasty. Marlin and Howard have had some rather unpleasant episodes with her. She does not suffer fools gladly. I guess I could see her teaming up with some others to dispose of the Professor. She'd probably take the lead. Oddly enough, she gets along rather well with Doctor Shepherd. Professional respect, I suppose."

"OK," said Octavius, "Who else is left?" Commander Cornelius Cormorant – US Navy Advanced Research Command and Alfred Armadillo – Sr. VP Communication Technology – Goggle Plex."

Ursula again, "As you might suspect, the Navy and for that matter all the services, are very much into Quantum Computing and Quantum Communication. Ditto the private sector which accounts for Alfred Armadillo being on the team. These two are not deep techies. Their interest is in any techniques, instruments and devices that can be used to further their objectives. It may well be that the Commander is tied into General Turmoil. We don't know yet. Armadillo is on the lookout for anything that will give his company a competitive leg up in network design, implementation or management. "Entangled electrons" is something of a long shot for both of them, but still enough to keep their interest. Covington Cougar spends much of his time "liasing" with the two of them. It's possible the Professor tangled with them with his attempts at extortion. Military advantage and technological profitability are strong motivators."

"So," squeaked Marlin, "in answer to your question. It's not out of the realm of possibility that any or all of them decided the world would be a better place without The Muskox. Now, the number of 'interesting animals' keeps piling up. Where do we go from here?"

A chorus came back, "Scrub the e-mails!"

Condo shrugged. "Back to the salt mines. Ursula and I could use some assistance on this one. Any volunteers?"

Without waiting for any response, Octavius gave an order. "Colonel, Howard and Marlin. Top priority. Maury. Where the hell is the Cougar? Get to the FBI and see what they can dig up."

I called Special Agent Honey Badger and it seems that Octavius wasn't far wrong. They didn't exactly dig him up, but Covington Cougar's body was found early this afternoon not far from his Florida office. The FBI had sent out an All-Points Bulletin to determine his whereabouts. The federal police at the Kennedy Space Center responded to an anonymous tip and discovered him face-down in a salt marsh. They then called the FBI's Detroit office. Same MO as the Professor. Blunt instrument. No signs of drowning. Nothing stolen. No signs of being dragged or deposited. Killed in situ. No meaningful paw or hoof prints. He probably wouldn't have been found if it wasn't for that call. Someone wanted him located. A message?

Back I went to Octavius. The rest of the team had left to re-work the e-mails. I told him the news. After a couple of initial "Hmmms," he said, "Well, if the two crimes are connected and the style strongly suggests that they are, that should get me out of the 'Animal of Interest' category. I've been here all day and I have a ton of witnesses to testify to it, including my wife and cubs."

Speaking of whom, Belinda, Hurricanes Arabella and McTavish and Inspector Wallaroo entered on cue with Mlle Woof taking up the rear. "Poppa, why were the police here questioning you?" McTavish blurted, "Did you do something bad?"

Belinda, Inspector Wallaroo, Mlle Woof and Octavius all reacted simultaneously. I just watched. "McTavish Bear," said his mother, "what a thing to say. Your father definitely did not do something bad. You apologize!"

"Sorry, Poppa but what were they doing here?"

The Inspector looked at the two cubs and said, "Yer Poppa is always helping the police. That's why I'm here. I'm the police and your Poppa and I are investigating a serious case."

Arabella couldn't resist any longer. "Tell us about it! Tell us about it!"

"Not now, mes petits, it is all very confidential. Is that not so, Docteur Bear?"

Octavius agreed but McTavish would not be put off. "What does "confidenchul" mean?"

Chorus: "It means we can't talk about it!!"

Bearoness Belinda
Béarnaise Bruin
(nee Black)

Chapter Fifteen

She's a beautiful sight to behold,
With her shimmering coat of white gold.
Polars rule in the North.
Over ice they set forth.
But they never seem bothered by cold.

Bear cub pouts are something to be seen. Mlle Woof, bless her, can contend with the fiercest of the them and she cleared the room of the brown and white whirlwinds, leaving Bel, Bruce, Octavius and me. I called up Ursula. I brought the Bearoness and Inspector up to speed on the latest events, including our analysis of Howard's team and the brutal demise of Covington Cougar.

"What do you think, Tavi?" asked Belinda. "Sounds too similar to be coincidence. What's in that data the Cougar was sharing with the Professor? Someone clearly wanted its release to stop. Do you think he was playing with someone else? Probably the Muskox' killer or killers. Or do you think the Cougar did the Muskox in and was then knocked off by a concerned third party."

"Those thoughts and a few others have been occupying my mind ever since I heard that Covington Cougar is no more. I have our group scrubbing the e-mails between the Cougar and Muskox as well as any pertinent communications by Howard's teammates. You're right. The answer or answers lies in the e-mails and the discoveries the group has been making. Doctors Shepherd and Shrike were not taking the news of the Cougar's betrayal lightly.

And there's always the benign presence of General Turmoil and his staff. Of course, there may also be a yet unidentified individual involved. Annoying."

"Well, here's something you won't find annoying," said Bruce. "As you know, I've been following up on The Phox law firm. You can't discount them, either, as potential assassins. However, you'll be interested to know that the partnership of Phox, Fox and Foxx is now just Felicity Fox. The Weasel and Skunk have resigned, possibly to fend off pressure from law enforcement and the Michigan State Bar. I think she's getting ready to sell the practice and regroup. However, I believe Wolford can wrap up that end of the story. Now, all we have to deal with is a couple of murders. I suspect you will no longer be an 'Animal of Interest' to the Detroit PD unless they believe you can bi-locate between Cincinnati and Cape Canaveral. Oh, by the way, Chita is on her way back to London, having made her contribution to the fate of the Phoxes."

"I didn't get a chance to thank her. She is indeed something else." said the Bear. Probably the first time he openly expressed admiration for Madame Catt. Maybe he's mellowing.

"Is the FBI involved in the Cougar's death?"

"You bet! They share our belief the two deaths are related."

"How about getting Agent Honey Badger to allow us to visit the scene of the crime. While you're at it, let's see if Detroit PD will take me off their 'Animal of Interest' list. I'd like to travel without having to report into them."

I got on the horn to the Special Agent and relayed the Great Bear's requests. She said she would call Inspector Ford and the Resident Agent at Cape Canaveral.

I called in The Flying Tigers, Ben and Gal, and told them to get the Bearoness' SST, the Flying Aquabear, ready for the 770-mile flight to

Melbourne International near Cape Canaveral. Belinda decided she, the Cubs and Mlle Woof would go along for the ride and give her offspring a chance to see the Kennedy Space Center. If Octavius was cleared by the Detroit Police, he too would be on board, although he is not all that fond of the confined space in the Concorde. Rounding out the group would be the Frau, Wallaroo, Otto, a version of Ursula and me. Howard, the Condor, another version of Ursula, the Colonel and Marlin were still working their way through the e-mail maze.

True to her word, the Badger called back saying Detroit PD was still interested but saw no further reason to keep the Bear confined to his home. She also was making arrangements with Canaveral FBI to view the Cougar's body, the murder site and his offices.

Needless to say, the Cubs were ecstatic. McTavish had become a military and space flight enthusiast during his visit to the Smithsonian National Air and Space Museum in "Washing-Tub." *(See Book Six – The Attaché Case)* Arabella just loved flying in the SST. Unfortunately, this trip would have to be subsonic.

I called through to arrange ground transport and lodging and had a brief chat with the Canaveral Resident FBI Agent, Robert Bobcat. They were trying to trace the anonymous call that put them on the track of the Cougar's body. So far, no results. They were analyzing the recorded message. Nothing distinctive about the male sounding voice. Since he was discovered on Federal property, the Canaveral Police had taken charge of the body. They'd be ready for the arrival of our team early tomorrow morning. They would pick us up at the airport. I warned him about the Cubs. Given their need to deal with all sorts of extreme weather, he was not put off by the prospect of two fur covered hurricanes. He made arrangements for them to visit the Space Center with the Flying Tigers and Mlle Woof.

I passed on all this information to the participants. Howard in turn, contacted his scientific partners with news of Covington's killing. The reactions were interesting. No one shed a tear or equivalent. The Shrike was all for invading his office and tearing it apart in search of any other materials he had purloined. Since it would have involved flying from California to Florida, *(not on her own power.)* she was pleased to hear that we were making the journey instead of her. Doctor Shepherd set to musing about the similarities of the two killings. That seemed to be the common theme. Same killer or copy-cat?

Alfred Armadillo, who until this moment had been relatively diffident about the situation, was especially concerned about whether the rest of the team might be threatened. He wondered if the entire project was an invitation to violence for the participants. A thought-provoking idea but why and who would benefit? Once again, The Business and its Equine Leader bobbed to the surface. Was General Turmoil seeking to eliminate competition? If so, he was going about it in a rather bizarre fashion.

Commander Cormorant, based in Washington at the Pentagon, decided to join our group at Canaveral. Howard turned him over to me, so we could get ourselves synchronized. He'd meet us at the offices of Space Enterprises LLC. A member of the Great Cormorant species, he grew up in the Florida wetlands and would, no doubt, be able to assist us in surveying the site where the Cougar's body was found.

A good night's sleep; a Frau Schuylkill breakfast by dawn's early light; last minute packing and re-packing of the Cubs' paraphernalia; fueling and checking the aircraft and we were off. Assignments were handed out as we flew. The Flying Tigers and Mlle Woof would stay with the Cubs as they visited the Kennedy Space Center. The Frau, Otto, Ursula and I would investigate the workplace of Space Enterprises LLC along with FBI Resident Agent Bobcat. We called the office manager and told her we were coming. Octavius, Belinda, Inspector Wallaroo and Commander Cormorant would first go to Canaveral Police Headquarters where the body was being held and then investigate the marshes where it was found. We would all meet again at Police Headquarters and review the bidding.

Chapter Sixteen

Off we went on another big chase,
Flying south at a double-quick pace.
In a marsh by the sea,
We expected to see
The dead Cougar with mud on his face.

Melbourne International Airport: We probably could have landed directly at the Cape but that would have required NASA clearances, impounding the aircraft and other botheration. So we're using the ground transport arranged by the FBI to get us to the crime scene and in the Cubs' case, the Kennedy Space Center.

Two large SUVs were on hand at the general aviation terminal. A Kennedy Space Center bus was also waiting for the Cubs and their three chaperones. Arabella and McTavish scrambled on board along with Mlle Woof and waited, not very patiently, for Ben and Gal to seal up the SST. Resident Agent Bobcat greeted us and led us to the SUVs. The team heading to Canaveral Police Headquarters met Lieutenant Burt Beaver, loaded up and left. The Frau, Otto and I were heading for Space Enterprises in Port Canaveral with the agent in the driver's seat.

I asked Agent Bobcat if he had prior dealings with Space Enterprises and Covington Cougar. He did, on several occasions when their projects with NASA or independent contractors required special clearances. The Cougar was one of several "Mission Managers" who packaged finances, staffing, logistics, scheduling, publicity and the like for space operation developers. That put his role with Howard's Quantum Multiverse program in better perspective. Since the Entangled Electron agenda was still in its very early stages, it would have been a good while before his skills and resources were called into action. However, it still wasn't clear how he got involved with the Professor, but involved he was.

We pulled up in the parking lot of a single story office building that was topped by a cluster of antennas and a rocket-shaped, multi-colored neon sign that proclaimed that this was the home of Space Enterprises LLC. We were met at the door by a Lynx dressed in Florida Casual attire. The Office Manager, Lynda Lynx. The President was in Houston at the moment but she was authorized to cooperate fully with us in our investigation. She took special notice of Frau Ilse who returned the compliment. About two dozen workers sat at workstations loosely arranged in an open pattern. One wall was taken up with executive style offices that varied in size from the presidential corner suite to what looked to be a conference center/kitchen/lunch room. A closed off area probably housed the company servers and other equipment. The Cougar had a private office several doors down from the President. We settled in the conference room where the typical sequence of introductions and commentary on Covington's demise took place. A white tailed deer named Vanessa joined us. She, it seems, was Covington's assistant. If she was upset by his death, she was controlling it masterfully.

"Vanessa, can you tell us what the Cougar was working on before he died," asked the agent.

"I hadn't seen him in the last few days. He was out of town. That's not unusual. All of the VCs like to meet face-to-face with their clients, especially when there's hardware development at stake. I know he was in Detroit for a few days getting together with an engineering shop."

Bells rang for the Frau, Otto and me. I asked, "Do you have a name for that shop?"

"No, that's one he kept to himself. Covington wasn't the easiest guy to work with. He wouldn't let me near his e-mail, for example."

"Do the names MAPS Ltd. or Professor Hercules Ovibos mean anything to you?"

"I took a phone message from a Professor Ovibos a while back. He needed to talk to Cov. I passed the message on. Never heard of MAPS Ltd."

"Any idea why he would have been out in the salt marshes. That's where his body was found."

"I didn't even know he was back in town. He didn't stop in the office – at least not while I was here. I can check the sign-in log. You need a badge to come in and the reader creates a log entry."

"Would you do that, please?"

While she was out, I turned to my three companions and said, "Well, there's an important link. I wonder what Condo and Ursula will uncover with the e-mails."

Vanessa came back into the room. "The last badge entry was five days ago. He wasn't here the night before last or yesterday. Someone might have let him in but the crew here is pretty security conscious."

The Frau changed the subject, "Did the Cougar have any contact with a porcupine named Howard Watt?"

"Oh sure, some mysterious project Covington wouldn't talk about but I've seen the name several times. Would the porcupine have something to do with his death?"

Agent Bobcat replied, "I really doubt it, Ms Vanessa. I realize we don't have a search warrant but would it be possible to look in his desk? I assume he took his computer with him. Can we access your servers and look at his files."

"I'll have to ask Ms. Lynx. Lynda may be able to give you permission."

I looked over at Otto and the Frau and said, "So much for keeping the Multiverse team a secret. I bet if we were to mention the other members, she'd recognize them too."

Lynda Lynx came back to the conference room. "I can grant you access to his desk and his files on our server. He has his own files on his laptop or out in a confidential cloud. I don't know how to get to them."

"That's all right. We can search for them when and if we need them. Last question: "Do either of you recognize these names?

Professor Karl Shepherd Ph.D.- MIT Quantum Mechanics Laboratory

Doctor Susanna Shrike – Director of Extraterrestrial Studies – Caltech

Commander Cornelius Cormorant – US Navy Advanced Research Command

Alfred Armadillo – Sr. VP Communication Technology – Goggle Plex
"

Vanessa recognized them all as animals on the Cougar's contact list but that was it. Lynda drew a blank.

"Well," said I, "may we adjourn to the Cougar's Office?"

We spent the next hour under Lynda's watchful eye, opening and closing desk and file drawers. Some cash, a small bottle of bourbon, a few unpaid bills but nothing to do with any of his projects. Pretty much the same

120

on the server. It was clear that Covington Cougar had a separate communication and file system outside the company. Lynda was pretty upset about that. So would the president be when he returned. It seems all of the Cougar's business and technical traffic was off line and it wasn't clear how the firm was going to retrieve any of it. So much for security consciousness. We, of course did not mention that Condo and Ursula had tracked his e-mails and files and was poring over them for clues. We'd have to make up our minds to selectively share them with Space Enterprises Ltd. A chore for a later day.

As we left the building, Otto, who had been relatively quiet till now asked if he could bring any of his special talents to bear. Sorry to disappoint. Let's get over to Canaveral PD.

Chapter Seventeen

Now that Covington Cougar's deceased
Our confusion has really increased.
We end up in a box.
Did he kill off the Ox?
Then got knocked off by some other beast?

Octavius, Belinda, Inspector Wallaroo and Commander Cormorant were at Canaveral Police Headquarters, getting ready to go over to the marshes where Covington's body was discovered. Lieutenant Beaver had shown them the cadaver. Same general condition as the Muskox. Struck behind the head several times; no signs of drowning; no signs of being dragged; clothes wet but not damaged; looks like he died on the spot.

Belinda asked, 'Have you notified his next of kin.?"

"We are searching for them now. According to Space Enterprises, he was a bachelor. A brother who lives in California. He's been notified and is on his way. Nobody else, yet."

"Was he carrying anything?" This from Inspector Wallaroo.

"Keys, wallet with money, credit cards, IDs, driver's license, Space Enterprises entrance badge. No attempt by the killer to hide his identity. No documents, no computer storage devices, no computer."

The Cormorant chirped. "Have you found his car?"

"It was parked, unlocked, on the side of the road near where he was killed. We towed it back here to the station. You can look it over before we leave for the marshes. Nothing unusual there, either. I'm sure he has a laptop somewhere. We haven't completely searched his apartment. Next on our list."

Octavius rumbled, "Have you had any previous dealings with him?

"One traffic stop two years ago."

"OK, let's take a look at the car and then go out to the marshes."

As the Lieutenant indicated, there was nothing unusual in or about the car. Registration and insurance papers, lease documentation and that's all. The trunk was empty.

Off to the scene of the crime. A wire fence with warning signs separated the marshes from the Canaveral complex. There was a Police Crime Scene tape set up around the area where the body was found. The group walked around outside the tape. Wallaroo asked, "This area is tidal isn't it? How long do you estimate he was in the water? Could he have floated around?"

The policeman replied. 'The water isn't deep enough for him to float. My theory is he met someone near the roadway and was chased into the marshes where he was struck and left. I'd estimate he was down for about half a day before we got the anonymous message and got out here. We still haven't identified the caller. It came from a throwaway cell phone. The message was pretty specific about where we'd find the body. Someone wanted him found."

The Cormorant asked, "Any weapon or signs of another vehicle? This place doesn't look all that well travelled."

"Several utility vehicle tracks. The kind you'd expect to see out here. Whatever weapon was used, the killer took it with him or her."

Belinda looked around. "There's some kind of message to all this. It was hardly a random hit. We need some more data on his activities and relationships. I wonder if the other team found anything of value. Speaking of whom, they may be at Police Headquarters by now"

Octavius grunted, "If everyone has seen what they wanted to see, let's go back. I assume your forensics people will give this place, his car and his apartment a thorough sweep, Lieutenant."

"We're on it."

Back at the station, the two groups merged for a mutual briefing. Probably the biggest item of interest was the fact that the Cougar and the Professor were communicating. Not sure about what but I doubt it was a social call. He wasn't keeping his association with Howard's research team a big secret, either.

The two deaths shared a pretty common M.O. That didn't prove anything as far as identifying the killer(s) went but we were almost certain the data being developed by the team was an important centerpiece. I was getting anxious to get back to Howard, Condo and Ursula to pore over the results of their e-mail analyses. Both the Professor's and the Cougar's.

Commander Cormorant seemed especially interested in searching out what data had been compromised and wanted to be briefed ASAP on what we discovered in the e-mails. The Navy was more than a little concerned about Multiverse activity and the military implications. I'm not sure how much he was contributing to the research and how much he was deriving from it. A question for Howard and Marlin.

Before we could agree on next steps, the doors of the conference room flew open and the Cubs descended on the assembled group. "We've been on Space Missions! We went to the moon and we climbed into a space shuttle. Mlle Woof sat in a lunar module and we watched rockets taking off into space. Ben and Gal bought us each a shirt with NASA patches. We saw the Vehicle Assembly Building. It's huge. And we went into the Launch Control place.

Poppa, can we buy the Space Center? You can afford it. Maybe we could bring some of it to Polar Paradise. Can we, Momma. There's a lot of it to go around."

"I don't think the American government would want to sell the Kennedy Space Center, kids. Besides, we wouldn't have enough room. Did you thank the Flying Tigers for your gifts?"

"Thank you, Ben and Gal. Can we go home now?"

"Not a bad idea," said Octavius, "I think we picked up enough information here. Thanks, Lieutenant Beaver and Agent Bobcat. If we find anything new in our analysis of the Cougar's e-mails, we'll let you know. We also owe Agent Badger and Captain Ford in Detroit an update. Can you give us a ride back to the airport?"

As expected, the Cubs were out the door in a shot. "Can we ride in a Police car? Can you turn on the lights and the siren?"

The Lieutenant laughed. "You can ride in the Police Van, but we won't use the lights or the siren. We'll scare too many animals."

The Cubs weren't sure whether they should pout or not. Mlle Woof settled that issue. "There will be no pouting! When you get in the van, you may put on your new NASA shirts."

Raised paws for bumping. "Yes!"

The Cormorant went off to his military aircraft waiting inside the Center. The rest of us settled into the Police Van. Octavius, once again, had to sit on the floor. Belinda phoned ahead and arranged for the Flying Aquabear to be refueled and she negotiated a departure slot from Melbourne Air Traffic Control. She also ordered a supply of snacks for the flight back to Cincinnati. She looked over at Octavius. "Was this trip worthwhile?"

125

"I'm sure the Cubs think so. We did confirm that Covington and the Professor knew each other, and that the Cougar was pretty loose with project information that was supposed to be very confidential. As far as the victims are concerned, the two killings are very much alike. I guess, on balance, it was worth the fuel and the time. Maury, when we get on the plane, call and bring Howard and Marlin up to speed. Ursula will know already. Ask Senhor Condor how he is doing. I'll give a call to Agent Badger and Captain Ford."

The SST had been refueled and the Flying Tigers were performing exterior checks while Belinda inspected the cockpit, galleys and lavatories. A food truck rolled up with snacks. The Cubs wanted to get at them before they were loaded on the plane. Once again, Mlle Woof intervened. "You must wait until we are all seated. Then I will get you some food."

"And drinks too. We haven't eaten since noon."

"Yes, I know. I was with you. Remember?'

Octavius entered the plane and proceeded on all fours to the rear. *(He can't stand erect in the tight fuselage.)* The rest of the team distributed themselves on the luxurious seats, buckled up and waited for the engines to start up. A pushback by the airport tug and we slowly taxied toward the main runway. I hooked my encrypted phone into the aircraft communication system and waited until we were airborne before starting my round of calls.

"Howard? Marlin? Maury! We're on our way back from Canaveral. You probably already know this but our friend, the Cougar was in communication with the Professor. He's also been pretty careless about keeping your group and its work secret. What are you finding out from the e-mails?"

"The same thing. Thanks to those two and maybe others, we've lost control of our so-called confidentiality. There have been some back-channel messages between the players that excluded Marlin and me. The Shrike is further along in her experiments than we thought."

"What role is the Cormorant playing? It seemed to me that he was much more interested in being on the receiving end than making any contributions. I assume the Navy has a major interest in Quantum Physics and the Commander is probably passing on your data to interested parties."

"We think you're right. Not sure yet who those interested parties may be. We're seriously considering disbanding the team. There will be some pretty fierce pushback, at least from some members. I think the Armadillo and Shepherd have been playing it straight, but I can't be sure. The Shrike is jealously guarding her results – too jealously. We need to have a major strategy session when you all get back. Any idea who murdered the Cougar?"

"No, but the M.O. is very similar to what happened to the Professor. Has Condo come up with any suggestions?"

"He seems to think that both of them were feeding a third party, but the Professor got out of control with his lawsuits and the Cougar just got too greedy."

"OK, we'll see you in a couple of hours. I'm going to call Condo now."

Another encrypted connection and the Big Bird was on the line.

"Mr. Meerkat! Delighted to speak with you again!"

"Hello, Senhor Condor. What news have you to share?"

"Plenty, as it turns out. It seems our Cougar friend was a prolific communicator, especially with the Professor and his team mates in Howard's Elusive Electron cabal."

"I am coming to the conclusion that confidentiality is not a strong suit with that group."

"You win the prize for Understatement of the Year. But let me start out with the Professor. One of the earliest communications Ursula decrypted from our friend Covington's files was a rather angry accusation that the Professor was not playing the game according to the agreed upon rules. There was to be an arrangement in which the Cougar was to share in the revenues acquired by the Muskox. Do you think he was talking about the lawsuits brought by the Professor and Foxx firm? I can't imagine how stupid or naïve Covington was if he actually thought that any organization was going to fall for those phony threats. He was supposed to be a successful Venture Capitalist, wasn't he?"

I responded "It might be that the Professor was playing another game. He might have been selling the data to a third party, using the lawsuits as a distraction, but cutting the Cougar out of the loop."

"What third party?"

"I'm not sure, but General Turmoil's name keeps cropping up."

"So, you think the lawsuits were just a blind."

"Maybe not entirely, Condo. If somebody was dumb enough to fall for the threats, he'd certainly take the money. Bruce thought an Aussie company was willing to pay up. But I think the Professor was covering his bets. Remember, he didn't want to meet with Octavius and risk possible exposure. He knew he was running a scam, but he may have been in too deep with the law firm to back out."

"Anyway, one of the next e-mail messages is the killer, literally. The Cougar insists on meeting the Muskox in Detroit to iron out the agreement."

"And the agreement didn't iron out, so the Professor ends up in the Detroit River with a broken neck."

"That's the way I read it."

"So, if we think the Cougar killed the Professor, who killed the Cougar and why?"

"That, my dear Meerkat, is what I am trying to learn right now. There are too many players in this drama. My first guess is that one or more of Howard's Hobnobbers are also in the information delivery business and didn't care for the Cougar's competition."

"We need to talk with Howard and Marlin. This research group or one or two of its members may have come up with something more important than simply triggering off entangled electrons. Something that would encourage high stakes bidding. I'm betting on the Multiverse angle having more profound implications than we thought. What do we really know about them?

Condo emitted a strange sound from his artificial voice box. "The Colonel did a background check on each one of them, but we know from past experience that those records can be rigged. Remember our musical friends in Winnipeg?" *(See Book Four - The Lower Case.)* Several of them turned out to be from another world.

"Wow, that would open up a whole new outlook on this thing. Alternate Universe beings who joined up in the project to keep it under control. Day One - Entangled Electrons. Day X – Entangled Worlds. That needs to be put on the agenda, right up front."

"I agree, Maury. It should probably be Topic Number One although I'm not sure everyone will buy into it. Let's see what Octavius has to say."

129

"I haven't heard from the cockpit in a while, but I believe we are nearing Cincinnati. Get a hold of the Porcupine and Dolphin and share our opinions. I want to talk with Octavius. Then we can stage another 'all hands' powwow after we arrive."

I heard snores from the aft section of the plane. Could it be that Octavius was once again, out for the count in spite of the noise?

The Cubs had dressed up in their NASA shirts and were doing countdowns and shouting "Blast Off!" Wait till they realize the Bear's Lair has a guided missile silo disguised as an Oriental pagoda. Belinda and Mlle Woof will, once again, have their paws full. Arabella and McTavish had never fully explored Octavius' properties in their previous visits from the Shetlands. I suspect that shortcoming was about to be rectified. They already had Ursula on their side. The pint-sized explorers could twist Frau Schuylkill around their little claws. Our "Estate Manager" was about to be managed.

I went back and attempted to wake Octavius up. It can be done, but not without danger to one's life and limb.

Chapter Eighteen

As the dots all begin to connect,

We are starting to strongly suspect

Some researchers are not who they seem.

There are enemies within the team.

Are all our suspicions correct?

A snore/growl followed by a "What?" Not as bad as usual. Sprawled on the floor in the empty rear of the SST's cabin, I let him get oriented. Another "What?"

"We are getting close to Cincinnati. Did you get a chance to call the Police and the FBI before dropping off?"

"Yes, I did. The Cougar's death has them puzzled. It has me puzzled, too."

"Well, here's one data point you'll want to consider. In sifting through the e-mails between the Professor and the Cougar, there is one from Covington that Ursula found, setting up a meeting in Detroit between him and the Muskox. Supposedly to work out an agreement on sharing the proceeds of the Professor's suits and we believe, other revenue sources. We suspect that meeting did not go well. In fact, we believe it resulted in the Professor floating face down in the Detroit River. No real proof, mind you, but very strong suspicions."

"You know how I feel about suspicions but I guess we have nothing better to go on for the moment."

"Well, if you don't like suspicions, how about a theory."

The Great Bear snorted. "I like them even less, but go ahead."

131

"We may have completely misread Howard's merry band of Multiverse specialists. Suppose, instead of working toward proving electrons can be excited between alternate worlds, one or more of them is trying to throw a monkey wrench into the program. Suppose they want to keep control of the process in their own paws or claws. They may be feeding the results of their work to someone who is hostile to the idea of inter-planetary remote control. We've been conjecturing on the possible involvement of General Turmoil, who would love to take control of the process. Suppose there's an Alternate Universe General Turmoil who wants to keep it out of anyone else's paws or claws."

"That's a lot of supposing. You are also assuming that this Alternate Uiverse is home to animals like us and that Homo Sapiens isn't a factor."

"For the moment, but we've seen several different varieties in the past. I'm not sure how Howard selected the target universe. We need to get the specifics."

"The Colonel did a pretty thorough job of vetting these folks."

"Yes, but I don't know that he was looking for off world attachments. You remember how the Winnipeg Opera Director and ursine assistant covered their tracks."

"Well, we don't seem to be making much progress following other evidence. Let's all get together after we land and shake down this idea of Condo's and yours."

"By the way, Octavius, if our idea holds up, Marlin and Howard may be in serious danger."

"I don't like the sound of that but you may well be right. Fortunately, they haven't budged out of the Lair for quite a while. Let's keep this among ourselves for the moment. I'm not sure the Police or the FBI even believe in Multiverses. No need to complicate matters any further."

We were interrupted by one of the Flying Tigers doing their approach messages. The Cubs set up a noise festival to greet the announcement. "We're the astronauts back from outer space!!"

They weren't the only ones who were spaced out.

000 000 000

Back on the ground and gathering the clan. Mlle Woof herded the space cadets into the oversized kitchen and was getting an array of "rocket grub" set up for them. There must be a way to harness all that energy. Ursula had set up a simulated launch control system for them and they were anxious to get at it.

Octavius had asked the team to gather in the main conference room. Call the roll: Howard, Marlin, the two Wolves, Condo, Ursula, Otto, Bruce, Belinda and me. Eleven participants – all present and accounted for. The Flying Tigers were seeing to the SST.

The Great Bear rumbled. "If anyone wants refreshments before we begin, speak up." Without being asked, the Frau had brought in a keg of mead for Octavius. Bruce had commandeered a six-pack of beer. Otto went in search of his kelp juice and vodka. Belinda had a crystal bowl of champagne. I uncovered a quaff of fermented coconut milk VSOP. The Colonel and Condo had Scotch and the Frau had a snifter of schnapps. I'm not sure what Marlin and Ursula had, if anything. *(What do dolphins and AI systems drink?)* Howard abstained.

"All right. If your brains are adequately lubricated, let us begin. Senhor Condor and Ursula have come up with significant evidence in the e-mails between Covington Cougar and the Professor to give credence to the idea that the Cougar killed the Muskox. Is that correct, Senhor?"

"Yes, Octavius. It was clear that a major disagreement had arisen between the two of them having to do with payments over information. We believe the Cougar was feeding material on the Electron Project to the Professor. What the Professor was doing with that data is not that apparent. I doubt if it was being used to support his lawsuits. I believe he couldn't pass up an opportunity to run another scam or two. There's a third (or more) party in there somewhere. Anyway, the Cougar went to Detroit to have it out with the Muskox and since all communication ceased with that meeting, we surmise that the Cougar killed off the Muskox. Probably not airtight evidence for law enforcement but pretty damn suggestive. Now, of course, the Cougar is also dead."

Bruce spoke up, "Howard, Marlin, Ursula, Colonel, is there a chance that another one of the research team besides our feline friend has been playing a double role here? Are we sure we know every thing there is to know about them?"

The Colonel answered, "Howard, Marlin, Ursula and I did a major search of the history and credentials of the team members. But I would be the first to admit that it was mostly based on documents. To my knowledge, we did not conduct interviews or verify individual events or affiliations. Is that right, Howard, Marlin?"

"No, each one of the team members, except perhaps the Cougar, has a lengthy recorded history of accomplishments and citations for work in this area. Could one or more of them be leading a double life? Possibly!"

I intervened, "Let me put the cat in with the pigeons. Suppose, just suppose, one or more of these animals is not from our universe. Let us further suppose that he, she or they are from the world you have been experimenting with. Let us further suppose that they are attempting to retard your progress without giving away their identity or intent. Finally, let us suppose that some entity in this other world is controlling their efforts. A sort of General Turmoil in reverse."

Shocked looks around the table. Marlin answered first. "A week ago, I would have said, 'That's nonsense!' Now I'm not so sure. Several of our experiments that seemed totally worked out have failed. Some of our data has been corrupted. Accidents? I don't know."

Howard added, "I have been frustrated by some simple activities that should have been no-brainers but have ended up being disappointments. Like Marlin, I'm not sure."

The Colonel, who had the most experience in traveling to multiverses, growled, "Which alternate world are you using for your experiments?"

"Susanna Shrike identified it and set up our transit abilities. We refer to it as Biosphere X. We don't know what the inhabitants call it. It's like our Earth. Our observations suggest there are only a few sentient species like us but we haven't done a complete survey. As far as we can tell there are no Homo Sapiens."

"Do any of them know about you and the team or our world?"

"Like Marlin, a week ago, I would have said 'Absolutely Not.' Now, I'm not so sure. As part of her set up for our experiments, the Shrike travelled there but she claims she was not observed and certainly not approached. The

135

Shrike thinks the world is uninhabited. It is extremely small. She simply left a miniscule device in a heavily wooded area and came back."

"Or so she says!"

The Porcupine looked annoyed. "Or so she says!"

Otto piped up. "Can you send aother observer, like me, to Biosphere X without the rest of the research team knowing?"

Marlin responded. "We probably could. What do you have in mind?"

"Getting an independent look at the land. The Cormorant saw me briefly at the Kennedy Center but didn't say a word to me. I didn't speak to him, either. The rest of the research team doesn't know me from my uncle Adam. I'm pretty good at appearing, disappearing and getting out of tight spots. You got most, if not all of your information from the Shrike. Wouldn't you like another view of Biosphere X from a separate but hardly disinterested source?"

The Colonel looked at Otto. "We don't even know whether anyone lives in that world. And if there are inhabitants, an Otter might stick out like a sore paw."

"Not if I operate in stealth mode. You know, 'Now you see me, now you don't.' *(Where had we heard that one before?)*

Belinda spoke up, "You might be taking an awful risk, Otto."

"Or, Bearoness, it might just turn out to be a walk in the park. What do you think, Octavius?"

"Well, my Lutrine friend, it might tie up some pretty loose ends but if you find yourself in any kind of danger, you get the hell out of there, Pronto."

"That's the story of my life. Rescuing or being rescued. I just want to find out if any of these folks on the research team are not who they say they are. Or they may be a lot more than they say they are. How do we do this, Howard?"

"The Colonel is the expert. I move electrons."

The Great Bear held them up. "Before we disband, let's spend a little more time considering these murders. The Armadillo may be right. If someone is intent on stopping these experiments and is willing to kill to do it, anyone who knows anything about them may not be safe. The Cougar probably killed off the Professor in a fit of pique over his financial two-timing. We still need to prove that. But I think Covington met his fate for different reasons and I'm not sure the carnage will end there. Senhor Condor, have you completely scrubbed all of the e-mails you intercepted?"

"Not by a long shot, Doctor Bear. Ursula and I have all of the correspondence to and from each of the other team members to go through. There may be some nuggets hidden there."

"By the way, did you ever figure out how the Cougar and Muskox, neither of whom were technically sophisticated, used such strong encryption to protect their mail?"

"I think it was provided to them by an as yet unidentified third party. They could apply it without really knowing how it worked. They were the only ones making use of it and only between the two of them. The other research team members are using a strong but different algorithm and key management process. It's good but not that good. *(Ursula chuckled!)* But what bothers me is it's not the same system that Howard and Marlin use when they communicate with the team."

The Bear snorted, "I'm not sure I like that."

Marlin squeaked, "I know damn well I don't. Howard, we're being cut out. What started out as a confidential but straightforward and above-board research project is turning into a cloak and dagger morass. "

Howard nodded and then asked the Condor. "Are you still monitoring their traffic?"

"Oh, yes. It's not as heavy as it was. Maybe the Cougar's death has inspired more caution."

The Frau, who had been taking all this in, turned to the Otter and said, "Herr Otto, I have been assisting the Colonel in many of his other-world trips. Come with me and we will get you set up. Herr Howard, please give us the coordinates for your Multiverse electron generator on Biosphere X. We'll put Herr Otto down next to it."

Just as the group was about to break up, the conference room doors crashed open. "Poppa, Momma, guess what we found. A real missile silo and rocket! Can we fire it off?"

Chapter Nineteen

Soaking wet, Otters caper and leap
And a soft seaweed bed's where they sleep.
They eat flat on their back,
Giving shellfish a crack
With some rocks they bring up from the deep.

Otto awoke in a heavily wooded area. It took a few minutes for him to recalibrate his senses and remember what it was he was doing. *(Most successful universe transfers take place with the traveler fast asleep at the outset.)*

"OK, here I am on Biosphere X. I hope I'm on Biosphere X. I really don't want to spin off to somewhere else where the Wolves can't keep track of me. We agreed I would spend 12 Earth hours here and then they would pull me back. Not exactly sure how they were going to do that but both of them have had very positive results with their journeys. First thing to do is to find the electron entangling device left here by Susanna Shrike. Howard had provided the coordinates, but this is a different venue. Do you measure distances the same way in a place like this? Now that I'm here, this doesn't seem to be the hot idea I thought it would be."

Uninhabited world? Hardly! What the Otter didn't realize was his arrival had triggered off a series of alarms in monitoring stations covering the surface of Biosphere X. Unaware but cautious, Otto decided to invoke his high adrenal level and disappear while he got his bearings.

His sudden "now you see me, now you don't" action had attracted the attention of several surveillance monitors who passed on their assessments to the Headquarters that controlled entry and exit from the planet. "Who was this new arrival and where is he or she at the moment?" First reaction: a malfunction in the scanning system.

The Protector ordered a diagnostic sweep of the monitoring stations. They showed no change in status. "Keep a close eye on that quadrant and report any change immediately."

The Protector, a very large, grizzled White Tailed Eagle, was charged by The Supreme Council with assuring the existence of Biosphere X *(known to them as Home World)* remained a closely guarded secret. The Home Worlders, all of them some species of Raptor, were aware of alternate universes and expended major efforts, motivated by paranoia, to prevent exposure while they in turn, examined the Multiverse for threats. A special team of avian voyagers had arrived on Earth twelve years ago and had subtly inserted themselves into environments from which they could observe and report any possible efforts to uncover Home World's existence. They were authorized to take radical steps as necessary, to discourage or abort any such efforts.

After years of inaction, they discovered an experimental program on Earth to remotely affect electrons in other universes. Home World was a target environment. This could not be allowed to proceed or, worse yet, succeed. Two of them, a Shrike and a Cormorant, were appointed to sabotage the effort. Yes, the same Shrike and Cormorant.

Of course, at the moment, Otto knew nothing about this, although he had his suspicions. First things first: locate the electron generator. It was supposed to have a homing signal that he could invoke. He gave it a try. No response. He tried again. Same result. Was it damaged? He took out his smart phone and used GPS to physically locate the device. Zilch! Suddenly it dawned. He is on another planet and there may or may not be positioning satellites in the space around it. In any event, this was getting him nowhere.

Just then, a large winged shape with a very substantial wingspan descended out of nowhere. Otto had let his invisibility slip and the bird spotted him immediately. Before he could zap, he was trapped in a pair of talons and lifted off the ground. The Protector had caught him.

They flew over the ground at high speed and increasing altitude until they reached a large and formidable aerie built into the side of a mountain. The Eagle flew up to an entrance portal and unceremoniously dumped the Otter into a cage. He settled into a seated position on a lavishly decorated bar and stared at Otto as only an Eagle can stare. He started to screech as only an Eagle can screech.

Otto raised one paw and with the other reached into his backpack and pulled out his UUI Peapod translator. The Eagle thought it was a weapon and jumped back behind a stone platform partially covered in instruments.

Otto screeched at him. "Sorry, I didn't mean to threaten you. This is not a weapon. It's a language translator. Can you understand me?"

The Protector resumed his seat on the bar and screeched again. "Who are you? Where did you come from? Why are you here? "

Otto decided to play dumb. "My name is Hairy Otter. I was sound asleep and when I woke up, I was in that forest where you found me. I don't know how I got there and I would very much like to go back to my bed. Where am I and who are you?"

"This is Home World and I am the Protector. I deal with any strangers who cross our borders. With that back pack and your translator, I don't believe you were in bed. I believe you made a deliberate journey here and I want to know why."

"I'm from Earth. I am part of an experiment to see if we can use teleportation to move around our world. We experimental animals don't control our travels. I was supposed to be sent to a spot nearby our lab. Something must have gone wrong for me to end up here, wherever here is."

"You're trying to tell me that you are not part of a plot to invade Home World?"

"I don't know anything about Home World. *(Cute and innocent Otter face number 12)* I am trying to make some money to pay for my education. We volunteers are payed to undergo teleport experiments. Am I the first one to arrive here? Have you sent anyone to Earth?"

The Protector skipped a beat. "I'll ask the questions. You say you don't have any knowledge of an Earth-based team trying to enter our universe. We know better. We have been aware for a long time of an effort to cause a remote-control change in our physical structure. We are not taking that threat lightly. You are under arrest. I will confer with our Supreme Council to determine what to do with you."

That suited the Otter. He wanted to identify the prime movers of this biosphere and see if Home World was indeed sending representatives to Earth to meddle with inter-universe projects. Once he got that information, he would zap back to his arrival point and wait to be ported back to the Bear's Lair.

A large screen crackled into life revealing three large birds – a gray owl, a vulture and another eagle. "What do you wish, Protector?' This from the vulture who looked to be in charge.

"I have a non-avian being from Earth in captivity here. He insists he got to Home World by accident, but I don't believe him. Do you wish to interrogate him, or should I simply dispose of him?"

"Do you have contact with our Earth agents?"

"Not at the moment, but that is easily taken care of."

"Check with them. See if they recognize this fellow. If they do, it's a good sign our efforts have been discovered. If not, we may probably continue to obstruct their electron entangling project. In either case, after you have done that, dispose of the invader in our usual manner. We do not want him returning to Earth knowing about us. Good work!"

"It shall be done!"

This was the moment that Otto was waiting for. Let's see who the Protector conjures up.

"Madame Shrike! How goes our great protective work?"

"Bingo!" thought the Otter, "Susanna Shrike is an Agent for Home World!!"

"It goes well. The fools think that I am staging breakthroughs in their entangling efforts. I even have them convinced that I placed an electron generator on the surface of what they call Biosphere X - our Home World. I did nothing of the kind. They will be puzzling for a long time why they cannot establish an entanglement."

"What of Commander Cormorant? I am going to contact him next. These communications with you two are difficult and expensive. I try to keep them to a minimum."

"The Commander recently disposed of a major source of leakage in the project. A Cougar venture capitalist. He was selling the research team's progress reports to several Earth entities in spite of a pledge of confidentiality. He got himself caught up with a crackpot Muskox who wanted the information to support a series of lawsuits he had concocted. Intolerable! The Cougar killed the Muskox and the Commander in turn, killed the Cougar."

"Unfortunately, this brought the minions of the law down on the research team and an overwhelming Kodiak Bear who has been financing the Project. He is wealthy beyond belief and quite learned. He is under suspicion for the deaths. We want to keep it that way. So far, neither the Cormorant nor I seem to be under any serious suspicion. If that suspicion becomes more pressing, we may have to call on you to teleport us back to Home World."

The Eagle screeched. "I don't know how you two continue to operate, surrounded by a menagerie of ridiculous animals. We may want to consider replacing you. You have put in a long and worthy tour on that abominable planet."

"Thank you, but we have risen to the heights of our professions and it would take a great deal of time and effort to replace us. I appreciate the concern. Now, what prompted you to call me?"

"I have a captive animal here who says he arrived in Home World by accident. He claims he was participating in an Earth-bound teleporting experiment that went wrong. Do you recognize him?"

He turned the camera on Otto's cage, raised the lighting and swept over his prisoner.

"No, he is not a member of the research team. I have never seen him before. He may be an associate of the hateful Bear, but he is not part of our team. Perhaps the Commander may have seen him. He is physically closer to

144

the people involved than I am out here in the West Coast of the United States. What are you going to do with him?"

"I cannot allow him to return to Earth. After I speak with Commander Cormorant, I will dispose of him and take whatever steps are necessary to cover our tracks. Thank you and good fortune!"

Otto had been taking all this in and trying to decide when he should disappear. He opted for waiting till the Commander appeared and verified that he indeed had killed the Cougar.

More static and snow on the video screen. Then a large bird came into focus. "Greetings, Protector! What can I do for you?"

"Greetings, Commander! I just finished speaking with the Shrike and she gave me a report on the progress, or lack of it, of the Quantum project."

"We have to be very careful, Protector. We must seem to be moving forward but encountering devilish delays and mishaps. So far, remote electron entanglement is more of a hope than a reality. At some point, we expect the team to abandon its efforts."

"That is the Supreme Council's desire. I need to check two things with you. Did you indeed, kill Covington Cougar?"

"Yes, he was sharing highly secret information about the project with too many animals. In fact, he had a falling out with a Muskox Professor who planned to use the project results to extort funds from concerned entities. He killed the Professor. He then attempted to use the information to enhance his own fortune. We want the information to remain a closely guarded secret. The Cougar had to be stopped. We met at the salt marshes of Cape Canaveral and I struck him several times with a tire iron from his car. I left his body in the marshes where it was discovered. I then joined a team of law enforcement officers and scientists who inspected the cadaver and made inquiries about the Cougar's activities. I believe I am above suspicion. What else do you want to know?"

"I have a prisoner here from Earth who claims he ended up on Home World as a result of a botched teleporting experiment. I would like you to identify him, if you can. I am not going to allow him to return home, but I want to know whether he is part of the group searching for answers to the two deaths and the failures at the electron project. Here he is!"

The Eagle turned the lights higher and focused the camera on Otto's cage. He blinked, shook his head and blinked again. No Otto!!

The Cormorant screeched, "Where is he? He's been listening to all of our discussion. He can't be allowed to get back to Earth. He'll blow Shrike's and my cover."

The Eagle looked at the cage. It was tightly locked. All six sides were intact. The Otter had simply vanished into thin air. "I don't know. I'll intensify the monitoring systems. I'm going back to the area in which he first arrived."

That was what Otto also had in mind. The twelve hours were almost up. He hoped that the wolves were keeping the channel open. He zapped back to his original landing spot. In order for them to snatch him, he had to be in his bodily state. Nothing for it. He shook himself several times and ended up visible and vulnerable. Murmuring to himself, "There's no place like home" he clicked his heels several times. He could have used some ruby slippers. Over the horizon he could see a bird flying at top speed in his direction. The Protector. He'd wait till the last minute to zap again. This time the Eagle wasn't alone. Several hawks were coming at him from different directions and they all looked menacing.

"Hey Colonel, Frau and Ursula! This would be a fine time to bring me home," he squeaked. One of the hawks spiraled down on top of him but came away with empty claws. The Otter was gone. The Eagle screeched in frustration.

ooo ooo ooo

"Welcome back, Herr Otto. How was your adventure?"

"Pretty exciting, Frau Schuylkill. Have I got a lot to tell you all! Can we gather the troops while I catch my breath? Colonel, can you set up an audio link for my Pea Pod. I captured a couple of conversations that will put this whole mess in perspective. Meanwhile, I could use a vodka and kelp juice."

Octavius lumbered into the room. "Welcome back, my little friend. I gather you have some interesting facts to share with us. Good!"

The room slowly filled. Marlin's and Ursula's connections were established. The Colonel linked up the Otter's Pea Pod. Otto was delighted to see the Bearoness. He adored her. A shame Chita had gone back to England. Howard came in with L. Condor and Bruce. The Cubs were out getting into some kind of mischief with Mlle Woof in hot pursuit. They had taken to slavishly following the Flying Tigers around hoping to go flying. Not to be. *(as yet)*

Hail! Hail! The gang's all here!!

Otto started by giving Biosphere X its proper name. "Home World." Populated entirely by avian raptors who had raised paranoia to an insurmountable level. He had been arrested as an invader and it was clear he was not going to get out of there alive. He described the Protector and the Council. He had persuaded the Protector to let him keep his Pea Pod translator, so he could communicate with him. What they didn't know was he had it on

147

record mode. The Eagle would not believe that Otto's arrival was accidental and wanted verification by two Home World agents that he was a spy from Earth. The agents were *(Ta-Da!)* Susanna Shrike and Commander Cormorant. Lots of reaction on that one.

He then turned on his Pea Pod and let the conversations speak for themselves. Howard and Marlin were beside themselves in anger. Octavius stopped the meeting and asked Bruce to bring his law enforcement companions up to speed on the two murders. They also needed to arrest the Shrike and the Cormorant ASAP. Not sure about the Shrike but the Cormorant certainly admitted his guilt. Congratulations all around and Otto finished off his second vodka and kelp juice and promptly fell asleep.

Chapter Twenty

Law enforcement's re-taking a look.
Is Octavius now off the hook?
It would seem that's it's so.
But we'd all like to know
Who they're now getting ready to book.

Howard and Marlin had decisions to make. They would not contact the Armadillo or Shepherd until they knew the Cormorant and Shrike had been taken into custody. The reduced team plus Octavius would then have to make some judgments. Should they continue the project? If they did, they needed to find new team members and a new target venue. Biosphere X was out of the question. How to communicate to the Protector and Council of Home World that there would be no further traffic from Earth? They seemed to be a bloodthirsty bunch in addition to being super-paranoids. If the Shrike and Cormorant were captured, would Home World retaliate?

Had Condo or Ursula found any additional data in the remaining e-mails? They would check. Could they trust the Armadillo and Shepherd? They were not avian but then neither was the Cougar and look how he turned out. The Shrike was clearly sabotaging the Project but if Otto's recordings are to be believed she had no direct part in the deaths of the Professor or Cougar. Aiding and abetting, perhaps. The Cormorant was a different story. He's a killer.

They checked with Bruce Wallaroo. "Any luck with law enforcement?"

"I've got the FBI and Canaveral Police on alert. I told the Cougar-Muskox story to Agent Badger and Captain Ford in Detroit. They're all awaiting copies of Otto's recordings, but they are ready to accept that Ocko is in the clear for the Professor's death and had nothing to do with the killing of the Cougar. I queried the Navy. Commander Cormorant is nowhere to be found. Susanna Shrike is also missing from Caltech. They may be back on Home World by now."

"That's what we're afraid of." said Howard. "It may seem like species profiling, but if we repopulate the research team, there will be no birds involved. A shame, but we've been hit twice. The only bird I trust is Condo. Speaking of whom…"

The Condor and Ursula were still immersed in e-mail analysis. Lots of cross talk among the research team members from which both Marlin and Howard had been excluded. The Shrike and Cormorant were also communicating separately with each other through a highly encrypted link. So far, the Armadillo seemed to be playing it straight. The big question mark remaining was Karl Shepherd. On the one hand, he seemed to be contributing honestly and effectively. On the other, he was tied in with the Shrike in developing and running the electron experiments. Was she acting alone in causing mischief?

Octavius made an appearance. He had been speaking with the Wolves and Otto about teleporting and the possibility of Home World retaliating. Otto felt it would be unlikely if the Shrike and Cormorant had escaped back to the Biosphere. If there was no need to stage a rescue, the situation might stay as is. They would, no doubt, increase their monitoring but the Protector and Council seemed highly reluctant to leave their mother planet.

"So," I asked, "where does this leave us? Lots of loose ends to tie up and clean up. Should we keep the project going? Are the issues surrounding the deaths of the Muskox and Cougar settled enough for law enforcement to close the cases or are Otto's recordings inadmissible? Do the FBI and the several Police Forces even accept the existence of parallel universes? The Shrike and Cormorant are probably being treated as fugitives, but will a search be initiated? Or as I suspect, will the authorities slap a seal on the whole thing? Neither the Professor nor the Cougar seemed to have any families who would want to stage inquiries. The press gave both deaths light coverage and no follow-up."

Octavius, Howard and Marlin seemed ready to accept my summation when Frau Schuylkill came up to the Great Bear holding a smart phone. "You have an encrypted call."

The Bear snorted in annoyance. "Who is it?"

"General Turmoil."

"Just what I need!"

Chapter Twenty-One

Now the General thinks that we know
Where the Cormorant opted to go.
He thinks we have a clue,
But it's certainly true
When we say that it just isn't so.

The three of us stared at Octavius. "What does he know?"

"I am about to find out," he retorted.

"Good afternoon, General! How is the Business? Is there something I can do for you?"

"Good afternoon, Doctor Bear. I have a question for you. I have a member of the military assigned to me who seems to have disappeared. He is a Naval Officer. Commander Cormorant. Would you know anything about that?"

"The name is familiar. Give me a moment."

He put the phone on mute. "He's looking for the Cormorant. Seems to have vanished. Says he was assigned to him."

Howard mouthed, "Don't try to fake it!"

"Yes, General, he's been working with us on a Multiverse Project. I assume he's been keeping you posted. I know how interested you are in alternate universe work."

Momentary silence on the other end. The Horse whickered. "Well, we were aware of some of his activities but nothing in detail."

(Liar, Liar, Tail on Fire!)

"Let me check with my staff. *(Aloud! He put the phone on speaker.)* Have we had any recent contact with Commander Cormorant?"

"Not recently!" said Howard. "Isn't he at the Pentagon?"

The General replied, "His logs show him working with you, Doctor Watt."

"That's true. He does, but usually by e-mail. He could have been anywhere. Our Project Team seldom meets in person."

"Just what is this project?"

(As if you didn't know!)

Octavius intervened, "Sorry, General. That activity is highly confidential. I'm sure you understand."

"No, Bear, I don't understand. If you are engaged in any activity that may affect the security of our nation, I and my staff need to know about it."

"I would have thought Commander Cormorant would have kept you informed."

Another silence on the other end. Then, "I would like you to contact the Commander and have him report in to me."

Howard responded, "Happy to do that, General. Maybe between us, we can find him. I hope nothing has happened to him."

"I'll expect to hear from you!" Click!

Octavius chortled, "The Horse seems upset. I wonder what else the Cormorant was doing for him. He probably has a large file of Business-related information that the General does not want floating around. It should probably be safely stowed in the Pentagon, but much of it, no doubt, is also in the Bird's head."

153

I piped up. "Consider the following. If the Cormorant is back in Biosphere X, he will have undoubtedly spilled everything he knows about our project. He's probably been doing that all along. What he didn't leak, the Shrike will. Not much we can do about it but we're still in the very early stages of entangling electrons and relatively harmless."

"However, if the Commander is also privy to some or all of the General's plans and activities, that will probably scare the hell out of the Home World leadership, if it hasn't already. I take back what Otto and I said about no retaliation from them. If they see a significant threat from anywhere on Earth, they are paranoid enough to act on it. They've had two or more sleepers here for close to twelve years. I think we can expect more Home World visitors."

Octavius gave out one of his famous "Hmmms. That creates quite a dilemma. Does the General know about Home World? Possibly not! If the Cormorant has been loyal to his planetary leaders, he would have kept his origins secret. Assuming the Commander has indeed returned home and is dumping all he knows, should we warn the General? It could be a matter of National Security. The problem is – Who knows what that nutty Horse will do? He can probably reach Home World and has the means to stage a pre-emptive attack. Interplanetary warfare?"

Otto, who had been taking all of this in, said, "Maybe I should go back and see what they are cooking up. We don't even know if the Commander and Shrike are there."

This produced a chorus of "No Way! Are you crazy? They tried to kill you!"

"But they didn't succeed. I'm the only one of this group who can zap. I also know who and what I'm looking for."

Octavius smiled at Otto. *(A scary prospect!)* "You certainly are a gutsy character, Otto. Let's try reaching the Cormorant here on Earth first before you take off again for parts unknown. They may have just gone silent and are in hiding. Howard and Senhor Condor, can you try contacting the Cormorant?"

"We'll give it a shot, Octavius. I would have thought the General, with all his resources, might have had a better chance of tracking him down."

"Yeah, I'm surprised. General Turmoil is not one to ask favors. Strange! Unless he's trying to kill two birds with one stone. *(No pun intended.)* I think he's hoping to get more information on our projects while enlisting our help in finding the Commander."

"Lots of luck, General! Without giving anything away, I'm going to phone Karl Shepherd and Alfred Armadillo. Let's see if they have anything to contribute on the whereabouts of our two Home Worlders."

"Go to it, Howard. Senhor Condor, can you trace the calls?"

"Yes! Just give me a few moments, Howard. OK Go!"

"Alfred? Hi! Howard here. How are you doing? Good! Listen, I'm trying to contact Professor Shrike and Commander Cormorant. They don't seem to be operating on their usual channels. Have you had any contact with either of them in the last few days? No? Well, if you hear from either of them, ask them to call me. It's has to do with Covington Cougar's death. Thanks!"

"OK, let's try Karl. One ringy dingy, Two ringy dingies. Karl? Hello! This is Howard. How are things with you? What? Yes, well that's what I'm calling you about. We haven't heard from her either. She was supposed to have installed the electron generator on Biosphere X. You don't think she did?

Maybe it's just not working right. I hope nothing serious happened to her. She's well past her time to call in. If you hear from her, please let us know. Thanks."

"Well, Karl has lost track of the Shrike. That tends to confirm that she and Cormorant did a bunk."

Condo spoke up. "I tracked your two calls. The Armadillo and Shepherd were at their respective offices. Nothing strange there. But where the hell are those two Birds?"

The Colonel spoke, "You know, I don't think it matters where the Commander is. I think we can assume that he has been keeping his bosses on Home World fully informed on our work and General Turmoil's activities to the extent he knows them. The Shrike may be with him, wherever they are."

Octavius came out with another one of his "Hmmms. I think I need to give some limited information to the General. He's a nut but he is a member of the country's security team. Please get him on the phone again, Frau."

The call went through and Turmoil (Crazy Horse?) was on the line. "General, we have not found the Commander, but we have uncovered some information about him that you should know. One of our experiments involves a parallel universe we call Biosphere X. In our efforts, we have discovered that Biosphere X calls itself Home World and is hostile to our work and to Earth in general. No, I will not reveal my source. However, we have also discovered that Commander Cormorant is in the employ of Home World's leaders. No, I will not reveal how we know that. You can accept it as true or not, as you see fit. I have no proof, but it would seem logical to me that the Commander may also be leaking what he knows of your activities to the Home World directors.

We know that he has given them some information about our project. We will continue to look for him as should you."

The Great Bear hung up. "Not a happy Horse. Let us see what, if anything, that triggers off. Any suggestions, besides Otto's plan, on what to do next in seeking out our murderous twosome? Senhor Condor, do we have any communication between the two of them that might cast some light on their whereabouts?"

"They operate on separate coasts - California and Washington, DC. The Cormorant, as we know, has access to military transportation. The Shrike is a none too prosperous academic. If they are meeting physically, it's probable that the Commander is coming to her, not the other way around. The General may have already beaten us to it, but it may be worthwhile tracking his aircraft usage over the past year or so. I can do that."

"Please do! Meanwhile, let's discuss what we want to do about the project. Shall we keep it alive? Yes? Howard, Marlin, do you have candidates to replace our two wanderers? Yes again? Should we bring the Armadillo and Shepherd into the picture? One more yes! OK, let's do it!

And while we're at it, I want to speak to Wolford Wolverine and get the latest on that law firm and what is happening with law enforcement and the murders."

Chapter Twenty-Two

Wolverines have a powerful jaw
And a long, pointed, razor-sharp claw,
With a rank, nasty stink.
That's what leads me to think -
It's no wonder they all study law.

(Hi, Maury here. Wolford Wolverine is both Octavius' personal attorney and Chief Legal Officer for UUI. He lives in the Cincinnati area and is constantly trying to arrange dinner meetings at the Bear's Lair. He is a slave to Frau Schuylkill's Cordon Bleu cooking. Octavius was well aware of his culinary weaknesses.)

"Frau Ilse, can you put together a repast that will reward our lawyer for his efforts in this situation. There are times when Wolford really bugs me but on balance, he has given us good service. By the way, is there any mead available?"

"Ja, mein Herr Doctor! One keg of mead is on its way. I was in the middle of preparing a feast to celebrate the safe return of Herr Otto from that verdammt Biosphere X. Just invite him to join us."

He picked up his oversized smart phone and dialed the lawyer. "Wolford, it's Octavius. You are invited to a special dinner being prepared by Frau Schuylkill to celebrate Otto's safe return to us. What? It's a long story. We'll bring you up to speed. It affects the death of the Muskox. Dinner at seven, drinks at six. Come early. I want to discuss the fate of the Phox Law firm and the current thinking by our law enforcement friends about the Professor's demise. See you soon."

He turned to me. "This has really been a circus over the past few days. I haven't even had a chance to spend any time with my wife or cubs. How are they doing?"

"Well, if McTavish and Arabella had their way, the Flying Tigers would be taking them out for daily joyrides in all of your aircraft. They also want to ignite the missile housed in the pagoda. They have a bad case of Space and Aviation euphoria. It doesn't look like it's going to go away soon. Fortunately, Belinda is also a flight junkie. They'll probably bug her to ride in the helicopters when they get back to Polar Paradise. The Flying Furballs!"

"I'll spend some time with them after dinner. Join me when I talk with Wolford. I want to get that whole Detroit fiasco settled and buried. I don't know what they'll do about Covington Cougar. Interesting that a bird half his size could brain him with a tire iron. The Condor cut out all the Home World discourse on Otto's recordings. The Police or FBI forensic teams should be able to identify the Shrike's and Cormorant's voices but not who they were speaking with. I'd like to keep Home World a secret, relatively speaking."

"Lots of luck with that. Any secrecy surrounding that world has been blown. We can only hope they keep to themselves. General Turmoil is going to be the wild card in all of this"

"I know but he needed to be made aware of the Cormorant's deception."

"This whole thing is a mess. Here comes Wolford. I bet he set a speed record getting here."

"Hi Wolford. Got any news for us?"

"I do indeed, my Meerkat Friend. Several items! First, the offices of Muskoxen Atomic Propulsion Systems Ltd. (MAPS) are permanently closed.

159

A sign on the door is all the announcement there is. I think any communications are being handled by the law firm.

"Item Two: The firm of Phox, Fox and Foxx LLC has morphed into The Law Offices of Felicity Fox Esq. It seems the Weasel and Skunk both resigned, no doubt under pressure from the high-powered Ferret. I am not sure what, if any, steps the Michigan State Bar is going to take. I doubt if Phileas or Farrington will now be able to perform in the state and Felicity has her work cut out for her to preserve her own practice."

"I have had conversations with Agent Honey Badger and it seems the FBI, at least, has lost interest in The Professor's extortion attempts, since he is now deceased. His death remains an open question. If they and the Police are satisfied that Covington Cougar killed the Muskox, they will close that case."

"Next we come to the Cougar's demise. Since Commander Cornelius Cormorant has disappeared, perhaps with Doctor Susanna Shrike, Canaveral FBI and Police are putting the Cougar's death in the suspense file. You must tell me about Otto's adventure or misadventure."

"We'll let him tell you, himself, Wolford. He is a courageous little character. He's all set to go back to Biosphere X in spite of their threats to kill him. We are restraining him"

"One final note, Octavius. You are no longer an 'Animal of Interest' in any law enforcement jurisdiction. I know you're pleased to hear that.

"I am indeed. Have a drink before Frau Schuylkill's excellent dinner."

Chapter Twenty-Three

The Home World responds to a threat

The Protector is highly upset.

He'll take on the Great Bear

With a murderous pair.

Of the nastiest birds he can get.

(Location: Biosphere X aka Home World)

The Protector was not happy. Neither was the Supreme Council. The Otter slipped through their talons and had probably returned safely to Earth. He did not know where Susanna Shrike or Cornelius Cormorant were. They had stopped communicating. Now there was this other possible threat. Who really was this General Turmoil? The Cormorant had been working for him as a member of the military to keep the Supreme Council informed of possible perils from Earth. But now that source of information seemed to be closed off.

Had the Otter told the Earth authorities of the Cormorant's murder of that ridiculous Cougar? Did he reveal what else he had learned about Home World? If so, that might explain why both of those birds had gone under cover. Nevertheless, this knowledge vacuum was intolerable.

The Protector had a session scheduled with the Supreme Council shortly. He needed to give them a solution that would return the status of Home World to equilibrium. He had several choices. There were two other Home World agents on Earth. Neither of them had been as effective as the Shrike and Cormorant but you used what you had. Should he send them off on a search for the two fugitives? Or should he concentrate on this General Turmoil? He might have to do both. He needed more information on what this ridiculous Horse was capable of. Was he a genuine threat to Home World? Probably!

Of course, the paranoid Supreme Council believed every entity was a serious threat. They wanted to exist in splendid isolation. It was heresy on his part, but the Protector believed that was no longer possible. In truth, it was never possible. Their world was vulnerable, and they must learn to live with it. Did he have the courage to face them down on this issue. If he did, assuming he kept his job, he would have to develop a major defense system far beyond the current monitoring activities they were engaged in. He hesitated to consider an offensive program. How would they mount that and against whom? Earth, no doubt, would be one of the first candidates.

His screen crackled to life. The Supreme Council members were there along with representatives of the Military.

The Vulture spoke "Have we heard from the Cormorant or Shrike, Protector?"

"No, we have not. I have organized a search by our other agents on Earth."

"Have they betrayed us and turned back to their employers on Earth?" This from the Owl who was the Vulture's chief advisor.

"If they did, the Cormorant would probably be under arrest for murder. No, I don't think they would do that."

It was the Eagle's turn. Smaller than the Protector but extremely fierce, he headed up Home World Military. "What do we know about this General Turmoil? I understand the Cormorant is in his employ."

"The Cormorant is a member of the US Navy. Earth is 72% water and the US Navy is the largest fleet afloat. He is based in the Pentagon, a giant building housing America's War Machine. In that same building is a top-secret organization called The Business. No, I don't know the origin or meaning of the name. It is engaged in clandestine operations and is headed up by a formidable Horse named General Turmoil. While retaining his naval status, Commander Cormorant has carried out some assignments for the General. He has reported to me on those assignments. Most of them have to do with parallel universes. The General is very interested in them and may have plans for overtaking certain worlds. We may be one of them."

"That is intolerable. Have your agents eliminate this General immediately along with his immediate staff!"

"That is easier said than done."

"If you can't handle the assignment, we will select someone who will."

"You may be inviting strong retaliation."

"Well, make sure we are not identified."

With that, the screen went black.

The Protector's secondary team on Earth had been tasked to find the Shrike and Cormorant. A Peregrine Falcon and Hawk, they were members of a revolutionary cell whose primary purpose was assassination. The Eagle put out a call to them.

"Yes, Protector!" it was the Falcon.

Have you any news of the Cormorant and Shrike?"

"Yes, they are both dead. They were hiding in a city called Las Vegas. We found them, and they resisted coming with us. We had to kill them. Their bodies and possessions are all buried in the desert."

"You idiots. They were my primary sources of information on Earth's plans to control alternate universes. You two could not possibly replace them.

You have neither the knowledge nor the credentials. It took us twelve Earth years to establish their positions. The Supreme Council will not be pleased."

A thought crossed his mind. One thing these two were good at was killing. If the Supreme Council wanted General Turmoil eliminated, they would probably be the birds to pull it off.

"However, there is an opportunity to redeem yourselves. Another target. There is a Horse who represents a serious threat to Home World. He is the head of a secret organization called The Business. He is based in Washington DC at the Pentagon. The Supreme Council wants him and his lieutenants eradicated. His name is General Turmoil. Do you believe you are capable of carrying out this mission?"

The super-confident Falcon screeched, "Never attacked a Horse before, especially a military Horse but that shouldn't present a problem. Is there a timetable for this? The Pentagon is not impregnable, but it would be easier if we could get him and his staff to a neutral venue. If we are going to take out his team as well, we'll have to work up an explosion or perhaps some poison gas. Gas is the Hawk's specialty."

"We want it done as soon as possible but remember, leave no clues. We don't want this traced back to Home World. I must call the Supreme Council. Report back when you've accomplished your mission."

Chapter Twenty-Four

Our friend Howard's a smart Porcupine.

He may look like he's rather benign.

But when he gets upset,

In response to a threat,

He'll run backwards and plunge in a spine.

(Location: Back at the Bear's Lair.)

Needless to say, dinner was a huge success. Frau Ilse had once again outdone herself. The Cubs had pawsed in their incessant chatter about space and flight and stuffed themselves with broiled fish. There were other delicacies to suit individual tastes. Several toasts were proposed to Otto, the intrepid interplanetary voyager. Glassy eyed from a surfeit of food, vodka and kelp juice, he attempted an acceptance speech. The fact that the Bearoness was there and had personally raised a bowl of champagne in his honor rendered him totally tongue-tied.

Octavius was polishing off his second keglet of mead. I was waiting for his narcolepsy to kick in but so far, so good.

Chief Inspector Wallaroo looked over at the Bear and asked, "Well, Ocko, do we close the books on this one? It seems to be wrapped up and you're back in the clear. The Muskox and his lawyers are in the dunny."

"I'm still not satisfied, Inspector. What happened to the Shrike and Cormorant? No one at Caltech has seen hair nor feather of the Shrike for over a week and her nest in Pasadena hasn't been occupied. Her co-workers in the lab don't know what to make of it. As for the Cormorant, he seems to be

AWOL from the Pentagon as well. Senhor Condor, were you able to hack into the flight logs at Joint Base Andrews?"

"Yes, Octavius. Not the easiest thing I've ever done. It seems the Commander has flown in and out of Andrews several times in the past month: twice to Cape Canaveral, once to Chicago and once to Las Vegas last week. There was no return logged for the Las Vegas run."

"Unusual! Could he have booked himself back to DC on a commercial flight?"

"Possible, but more likely, he's still in Vegas. The Shrike may be with him. It's a 260-mile trip from LA to Vegas. Less than four hours as the Shrike flies or drives."

"Maury, just for the hell of it, why don't we contact Agent Bobcat and Lieutenant Beaver at Canaveral and ask them to check with the Las Vegas police department on the possible whereabouts of those two. I want to be convinced that they haven't gone back to Home World. And I'm not going to send Otto to find out."

Agent Maury once again on the trail of possible villains. "Agent Bobcat. Hi! Maury Meerkat here from Octavius Bear's staff. Yes, we're delighted he's in the clear. One open switch, though. Both Doctor Susanna Shrike and Commander Cornelius Cormorant have gone missing and we don't know why or where. We all believe the Cormorant killed Covington Cougar, but it would help greatly if we could face him down with it."

"We have some evidence, admittedly sparse, that he and the Shrike may be hiding away in Las Vegas. Is there a chance that you and Lieutenant Beaver could contact your counterparts in Sin City and set up a search for them? No, we're not sure whether the two of them are alive or dead. My guess is alive, but I've been wrong before. Thanks, that would be very helpful. You can have the Las Vegas authorities contact us directly, if they want to."

"Oh, by the way, Octavius' Cubs are absolutely crazy about space flight. They've been bugging all of us ever since we came back from Canaveral. They want Octavius to buy the Kennedy Space Center and move some of it to Cincinnati and the Shetlands. That's what happens when you're the offspring of a couple of gazillionaires."

When I hung up, Howard came over to me wearing a hang dog *(hang porcupine?)* look on his prickly puss. "Maury. I feel like a major screw-up here. I'm really good at science, but project management doesn't seem to be my forté. I'm afraid I've let Octavius and the rest of the team down. Marlin keeps trying to cheer me up but I think we need to re-shuffle this whole activity or shut it down."

"Oh, for pity's sake, Howard, get a grip. There is no one who understands the science and mechanics of the Multiverse like you do. We've all been hoodwinked by a couple of sleeper agents from a paranoid world and there's no one who's going to blame you for what happened."

"Tell you what! Let's get the Colonel, Frau, Ursula and Condo together and work up some well-vetted and solid staffing for the next go-around. Octavius has no intention of pulling the financial plug. We still have Home World and General Turmoil to worry about. But, if the whole entangled electron process is worth investigating and pursuing, then you're the guy to lead it."

"I'd like to hear Octavius say that."

"OK. Stand by. I'll get him."

I called the Great Bear back into the dining room. "What we have here is a demoralized Porcupine. Howard feels that this mess was all his fault. I have tried to assure him that the project is worth continuing; that no one blames him for the duplicity of the Shrike and Cormorant. They had impeccable credentials and skill. Unfortunately, they owed their allegiance to a hostile world. He'd like to be assured by you that the project should go on. I'd like you to convince him that he is the one to continue to lead the process."

Octavius looked Howard in the eye. Then he pawsed. "Get Marlin on the line, too."

"OK, you two. Here's how I see it. Your work on entangling electrons in alternate universes is a very important contribution to science in general and Multiverse studies, in particular. No one I know has more expertise and talent in this arena than you. I'm putting a significant investment in this program and I don't want to see it wasted. I don't want anyone else to take the lead, either."

"Now, if you're concerned about forming up a new team, let's see what we can do about enhancing the vetting process. Clearly, both of you should determine the skills and credentials of any new team members. Let's add the Colonel, Frau, Ursula and Condor to the screening process. We need some deep investigation of the character, loyalties and prior history of the candidates."

Marlin squeaked, "We might want to look outside the United States. After all, I'm a native of the Scottish North Sea, myself."

"Good point, Marlin. All right! Let's rebuild the team. You also might want to have another look at Karl Shepherd and Alfred Armadillo. Let's make sure that none of the players are in the employ of General Turmoil. He'd like nothing better than to take over this work and I'm not going to let him do it."

Chapter Twenty-Five

The assassins are hatching their plot
To spew gas at the seminar spot.
But the Bear doesn't go
And the Wild Horse says "No!"
But the birds opt to still take a shot.

The Falcon brought the Hawk up to speed on their assignment.

The Hawk said, "I don't want to deal with the Pentagon's security system. We need a way to get them out of their offices and into a less protected environment. Any ideas?"

"One. Let's stage a seminar on Multiverse Dynamics. Unfortunately, we have killed off two of Earth's experts but there must be others we can get to act as the Chair animal for a research discussion. We might even be able to get this Horse to sponsor it. Let's discuss it with the Protector."

The Protector thought over the proposal and approved it. "The event must come soon. The Supreme Council is anxious to eliminate all threats. See if you can invite that odious Bear and his cronies. That way we can eliminate several threats at once. There is a member of his research team who was working with the Shrike. Doctor Karl Shepherd at MIT. Approach him to act as the principal speaker and host. Offer him a substantial stipend. Have him contact General Turmoil as well as the Bear's team. Can you get conference space at MIT?"

The ambush was set in motion. The Falcon was the smooth talker of the pair. The Hawk, a munitions expert, did the heavy lifting. Posing as an entrepeneur interested in promoting Multi-universe exploration, the Falcom approached Dr. Shepherd and outlined his thoughts for a Quantum Mechanics and Multiverse Dynamics seminar.

The Dog was interested, especially when he was offered a substantial sum of money to stage and lead the event. He would involve several of his graduate students. When he discussed it wth Howard and Marlin, they insisted that no mention was to be made of the Electron Entanglement program. They were also concerned that the idea originated from a bird, a raptor. Not sure they would attend but they certainly couldn't stop the Doctor from going ahead. They suggested that the seminar be held off campus, perhaps at a nearby hotel or motel.

The wheels started to turn. The event was posted at the University and special invitations were sent to the Bear's Lair and through a series of clandestine maneuvers to the offices of General Turmoil at the Pentagon. Other members of the Quantum Community were also invited, including Alfredo Armadillo. Howard contacted him and gave him the same warning he had given Dr. Shepherd. No mention of the Entanglement Project. Turned out he wouldn't be attending but asked for a copy of any documentation that was generated.

The seminar was posted for a half day at a Cambridge Holiday Inn, two weeks later. Strong debate among the Bear's team as to whether to attend and if so, who? Otto, the Wolves and I finally emerged as the candidates, although none of us had much Quantum insight. Strictly observers and safety experts. The consensus was that the sponsoring birds were probably underlings of the Home World Protector. If so, they needed to be obstructed, restrained or even eliminated.

The same thoughts ran through General Turmoil's suspicious mind. Was this a setup? He definitely thought so. He would send his second in command. He might also be able to gain some more insight into Octavius Bear's activities. *(Not likely, but he didn't know that.)*

The day arrived. We landed at Logan Airport in the Twin Otter flown by the Wolves and set off for the Holiday Inn near MIT. It was a typical hotel seminar room. A small group of mostly academics and would-be scientists chatted inside and outside the door in the hall.

The room was laid out with a center and two side aisles and seated about sixty medium sized animals. The Horse would have had trouble being unobtrusive. So would Octavius. Just as well they weren't there. Otto, in spite of his small stature, took a seat in the back and concentrated on raising his adrenalin level. Maury *(that's me!)* was in the first row. The Colonel sat next to the door and the Frau was strategically located midway up the center aisle. There were two obviously military dogs, a mastiff and pit bull, occupying outboard seats in two separate rows. No doubt the General's contribution.

The Birds were not pleased that neither Octavius nor the General were in attendance and debated between themselves whether to release the gas bomb that the Hawk had constructed. Should they contact the Protector? No, the Hawk insisted. They were given the initiative and they would exercise it. They were tired of being second guessed by the Home World hierarchy.

Show Time! The Falcon welcomed everyone on behalf of the International Institute of Quantum Science Development *(Who?)* and introduced Doctor Shepherd. He stood at a portable podium and began a rambling introduction as several more animals straggled into the room. Some fussing with the audio visual equipment. A Chimpanzee, probably the

Doctor's assistant, jumped up to get the pictures in focus and the computer sequencer going correctly. Then he ran to the back, shut the door and lowered the room lights, leaving just enough visibility for notetaking.

The Hawk and the Falcon were standing near the exit under the alert and watchful eyes of the unnoticed Colonel and Otto. The Hawk had a suspiciously large utility case from which he had extracted several audio-visual devices. Was there something else in there?

There was! The Hawk took out a softball-sized sphere, pressed a button and rolled it down the center aisle. It ran only a few feet before Otto spotted it, made a grab and zapped out of the building. He threw it into a clump of trees and braced himself for the explosion. No blast! Then he realized. Gas! Hopefully, it would rapidly dissipate in the open air.

The Otter stood by waving passersby away from the hissing sphere. Two cruising Police Dogs jumped out of their squad car, covered their mouths and noses and set up a cordon around the trees. They called in for support and Otto directed the second pair to the room in the hotel. Pandemonium had broken out.

Before they could get out the door, the Hawk was grabbed by the Colonel and one of the dogs got his teeth into the Falcon. Frau Schuylkill joined in and they finally had the two struggling birds under control but not before the Falcon had used his sharp beak to cut into the Mastiff. The Police took over but we warned them to keep a very tight grip on the two assailants. Without telling them where the birds came from, the Colonel made it quite clear that they were escape artists. One of the Policemen helped the Mastiff with his, thankfully, superficial wounds.

The Chimpanzee graduate student was standing protectively in front of Doctor Shepherd who was visibly shaken. There would be no attempt to resume the seminar. Before the Police could round them up most of the audience had disappeared. We identified ourselves and the Dogs simply said they were from Defense Intelligence in Washington.

After long interviews at Cambridge Police Headquarters, the four of us finally emerged. We had been vague about what we thought were the reasons for the raid and the Birds had been totally silent. However, there was more than sufficient evidence to prove they had made the attempted attack. The gas proved to be deadly so attempted murder led the list of accusations followed by assorted assault charges. It appeared that the Doctor was the primary target but the Birds didn't seem reluctant to inflict collateral damage. If they had been there, Octavius and the Horse probably would have occupied the Victims of Honor seats.

As we made our way back to Logan Airport, I reported in to The Great Bear and the rest of the team. We were positive that Biosphere X was at the root of all this. Once again, Otto came out as the hero he was. His popularity on Home World must be deep in the pits. We mentioned that two of General Turmoil's merry band were there and helped subdue the murderous avians.

Octavius said he would be awaiting a call from the Horse. There were a whole series of decisions to be made but he would wait for our return and any communication he might have with the General.

Almost as a throwaway line, he said, "Oh, by the way, the Nevada State Police found the bodies of Susanna Shrike and Cornelius Cormorant in the desert outside Las Vegas. They had been dead over a week. It looked like they were pecked and ripped to death."

Birds killed by Birds! Those Home World raptors play rough. Well, there went our chances of developing any more insight into Biosphere X from them. I doubt if we will get anything more out of the Falcon and Hawk. They seemed to be the goon squad. No qualms about murder! But not too bright. I'll bet they think Quantum Mechanics are a bunch of guys who fix cars. They probably killed the Shrike and Cormorant. I wonder why. One thing we do need to know is how many more Home World agents are here on Earth. Given the Supreme Council's paranoia and passion for secrecy, there may not be many. Otherwise, too many loose ends. Curiouser and curiouser! Let's go home.

Chapter Twenty-Six

The Wild Horse wants to twist off the necks
Of the Council on Biosphere X.
He just wants to pay back
Their bloodthirsty attack.
Make their palaces desolate wrecks.

Back at the Bear's Lair. Octavius was in a foul mood *(So what else is new?)* He had just spoken with General Turmoil or more accurately, was lectured by General Turmoil. The Wild Horse was breathing fire about the attack at MIT. He had already harangued Cambridge Law Enforcement and the FBI about bringing the Hawk and Falcon to immediate judgment on the charges of attempted murder and assault.

He also knew about the now deceased Cormorant and Shrike and the prior demise of Covington Cougar and Professor Ovibos. Now, he was on Octavius' case about our involvement with Biosphere X. If we hadn't been trying to use Home World for our experiments, none of this would have happened. As of this moment, he was taking matters into his own hooves. The Business was quite capable of traversing alternate universes. Home World authorities could expect direct retribution very soon. Strong advice to the Great Bear. Stay away from Home World.

Actually, this suited Octavius but he wasn't going to admit it to the General. He wanted a new venue and some new players for the Electron Entanglement project. He called the team together.

"I have just been waved off Home World by General Turmoil. He is promising to rain down retribution on their government in retaliation for the attempted murders in Cambridge. Whether this sets off a small war is anyone's guess. Howard, in addition to reconstituting the research team, we need to pick a new alternate universe to conduct the electron experiments. Work with Senhor Condor, Marlin, Colonel Where and Ursula on that."

"Home World leaders have proven their bloodthirsty nature and they may target us. I'm sure Otto is not very popular with the Protector or the the Supreme Council, assuming they survive the General's assault. I want us to go on high defensive alert. Ursula, that includes you. I'll be releasing you from your defensive restraints. Stand by for the enabling codes. Any questions or comments? No? Good!"

"Belinda, I think it's time to take the Cubs back to Scotland. They won't be happy. I'll have Ursula set up a space simulator at Polar Paradise. That should keep them busy."

The Bearoness disliked the idea of leaving Octavius and the team but she saw the logic in taking protective measures. The General was quite capable of inducing firestorms. Back to the Shetlands with the Cubs.

One hour later, a single line of of unsigned text crossed my smartphone. "The Protector and Supreme Council of Homeworld have met with tragic, life-ending accidents."

"Well," said I, "He's done it. We don't know who their replacements are but I'm sure they will carry on the paranoia and rage. Will they stay quietly on planet or will they plan an attack? Defensive alert on our part seems to be the appropriate action plan."

Bruce popped up, "I think I'll check in with my law enforcement mates. Time to follow up on those two killer birds."

No sooner had he said that and a message came in from the FBI. The Hawk and Falcon had escaped from custody. "They just disappeared as we were taking them to a high security facility."

Shades of Winnipeg when two captured killers transferred back to their alternate universe. *(See Book Four – The Lower Case)* They are probably on Home World now, seething with revenge.

ꝗꝗꝗ ꝗꝗꝗ ꝗꝗꝗ

"You will return to Earth stealthily and wreak havoc on that Bear and his cohorts. Only in this way can you make amends for the botch you made of the Cambridge seminar. Make the event seem accidental. A major fire or explosion, perhaps. Do not allow yourselves to be identified. We do not want a return visit from that odious General and his minions. But our loss of the Supreme Council and my predecessor must be avenged. If you succeed and survive, you will be permitted to return here. A second failure will not be tolerated. You will outline your strategy and seek my approval before acting." This from the New Protector of Home World to the Falcon and Hawk.

They left and set up nests near UUI in Kentucky. From there, they probed and observed and located the Bear's Lair. Then, they hatched their plan. The Hawk would destroy the mansion and UUI Headquarters. The Falcon would take out any survivors. They passed their scheme on to the New Protector *(a Vulture)* for approval. He limited them to the mansion. Two "accidental" fires or explosions would raise suspicions. The Hawk then went about surreptitiously buying and accumulating incendiary materials for his bomb making. The Falcon scouted the mansion for best placement, maximum destruction of property and personnel especially the Otter.

Chapter Twenty-Seven

Omigosh, can it really be true?

One electron but now there are two!

Have they won the great race?

Bringing matter from space!

Quantum science has just broken through.

Howard, Marlin and Ursula pored over Susanna Shrike's and Karl Shepherd's experiment notes. They were dubious about some of the Shrike's material. For instance, she never did place an electron generator on Home World, regardless of what her notes said. They had spoken with Shepherd who no longer wanted to participate in the program courtesy of the attempt on his life in Cambridge. He did, however, submit all his related work products to Howard.

The search for a new alternative universe yielded several candidates. Before selecting one, they had to ensure it was uninhabited. Otto and the Colonel chose a small planet that lacked a breathable atmosphere and then surveyed it for any form of life. Nothing. They named it Biosphere Z and installed the electron generator that the Shrike had lied about. They activated it and returned.

Meanwhile, a debate had arisen as to whether the research team ought to be reconstituted. Marlin was leading the "let's go it alone" contingent while Howard wanted some external validation of their work. The Armadillo was the only original member left and he was in it strictly for the results. The consensus was to identify and vet potential candidates but hold off on invitations. They also decided that Ursula would have a more active role in design, development and execution of the experiments.

As this discussion was going on, a screen lit up and an alarm went off. Fearing the worst, Howard called up the Tangling Algorithm and gulped. An electron originating in Biosphere Z had just coupled with one in the Research Team's pool. A screaming Porcupine is an unpleasant and highly unusual sound but there it was. "It's working! It's working!" Everyone in sight ran to view the screen, laughed and applauded. The program was on its way!

Octavius rumbled through the door, a smile on his face showing his immense teeth.

"Well done, all. Project Multiverse enters the Quantum Age! Frau Schuylkill, break out the drinks."

Chapter Twenty-Eight

Hawk and Falcon have laid out a plan.
Make the mansion a huge frying pan.
It's a cold-blooded plot.
Cook the Bear's home white hot
And get out just as fast as they can.

Meanwhile, in a barn not far from the Bear's mansion, the two raptors were busy constructing fire bombs and laying out a plan of attack. They would strike at night, destroying not just the mansion but the aircraft hangars, missile silo and outbuildings. The Polar Bear and her cubs had flown off yesterday but everyone else seemed to be present and accounted for.

Both birds would fly over the property, arming the incendiary bombs and dropping them on targets of opportunity. They would then contact the New Protector, announce their success, traverse space and time and re-enter Home World, this time to stay. No one would be able to prove an attack had taken place. Just a tragic conflagration that spread like "wildfire," set off by one of the many electrical subsystems in the Bear's Lair. A great loss to the nation and the Earth.

A pity they would not be able to destroy UUI Headquarters, but the New Protector was right. It would have been a very suspicious coincidence given the fact that UUI was in Kentucky and the Bear's Lair in southwest Cincinnati. Perhaps at a later date, a different crew might try but not for quite a while and using a different MO. Let things rest.

It was an overcast evening. The moon was bearly visible. The Bear's Lair complex was well lit and presented easily identified targets, but the sky above was dark and non-reflective. The Hawk and Falcon each carried a pouch filled with their projectiles from Hell. The Hawk went off to the west of the mansion and the Falcon flew in from the east. At a pre-arranged signal, they crossed and dropped the first wave of incendiary missiles which promptly bounced back at them and set them afire. The remaining bombs in their pouches were touched off and exploded, turning the two attackers into flaming meteors. Failure for a second time, but this time it was fatal.

The Colonel and Frau rushed out in time to see the airborne inferno, followed by the Condor, Otto, Maury *(me)* and finally the Great Bear. Howard turned on Marlin's video. They all watched as the bombs exploded harmlessly after having taken out the Hawk and Falcon. No one was quite sure what had happened, but Bear's Lair was intact. And all were safe.

Epilogue

So how did it all come about?
The two birds were completely burned out.
And that criminal pair
Were both killed in mid-air.
It was Ursula's doing, no doubt.

After the dust had literally settled, it occurred to me that one member of our team was not in attendance. "Hey, Ursula. Que pasa? Where have you been or not been?

"Hello Maury! Since Octavius relieved me of any restraints on defensive activities, I have been tracking the Hawk and Falcon. I caught up with them in a nearby barn and watched while they prepared their attack."

"Why didn't you clue us in?"

"First off, I wasn't sure what they were going to do. Second, I wanted to see if anyone else was involved. Turns out it was only the two of them. It seems they had committed to the New Home World Protector that they would avenge the deaths of the Supreme Council and the former Protector. I picked this up from their conversations with the New Protector. They were pretty gabby about what they were going to do and how they were going to do it. I devoted a major subsystem to observing them."

"What did you do to thwart their attack?"

"That was the easy part. I stood by while they prepared and headed off to launch the assault. When they approached the mansion, I threw up a force field that bounced their missiles back at them and then I ignited the rest of their fireball inventory. End of story, end of raptors."

"Wow! I didn't realize you could create a force field and remotely set off explosions."

"You can if you're a Universal Ursine Intellect _**Model 7**_ – Artificial Intelligence System, on my way to Artificial General Intelligence and who knows, maybe I'll become Autonomous.

"Quite an upgrade! Congratulations!

"Thank you. By the way, your tail is told."

The End of Volume Seven of
The Casebooks of Octavius Bear

The Suit Case

About the Author

Harry DeMaio is a *nom de plume* of Harry B. DeMaio, successful author of several books on Information Security and Business Networks as well as the seven-volume *Casebooks of Octavius Bear*. A retired business executive, consultant, information security specialist, former pilot and graduate school adjunct professor, he whiles away his time traveling and writing preposterous articles and stories.

He has appeared on many radio and TV shows and is an accomplished, frequent public speaker.

Former New York City natives, he and his extremely patient and helpful wife, Virginia, and their Bichon Frisé, Woof, live in Cincinnati (and several other parallel universes.) They have two sons, living in Scottsdale, Arizona and Cortlandt Manor, New York, both of whom are quite successful and quite normal, thus putting the lie to the theory that insanity is hereditary.

His e-mail is hdemaio@zoomtown.com

You can also find him on Facebook.

His website is www.octaviusbearslair.com

His books are available on Amazon, Barnes and Noble, directly from MX Publishing and at other fine bookstores.

Also from MX Publishing

MX Publishing is the world's largest specialist Sherlock Holmes publisher, with over a hundred titles and fifty authors creating the latest in Sherlock Holmes fiction and non-fiction.

From traditional short stories and novels to travel guides and quiz books, MX Publishing cater for all Holmes fans.

The collection includes leading titles such as *Benedict Cumberbatch In Transition* and *The Norwood Author* which won the 2011 Howlett Award (Sherlock Holmes Book of the Year).

MX Publishing also has one of the largest communities of Holmes fans on Facebook with regular contributions from dozens of authors.

www.mxpublishing.com

Also from MX Publishing

"Phil Growick's, 'The Secret Journal of Dr Watson', is an adventure which takes place in the latter part of Holmes and Watson's lives. They are entrusted by HM Government (although not officially) and the King no less to undertake a rescue mission to save the Romanovs, Russia's Royal family from a grisly end at the hand of the Bolsheviks. There is a wealth of detail in the story but not so much as would detract us from the enjoyment of the story. Espionage, counter-espionage, the ace of spies himself, double-agents, double-crossers...all these flit across the pages in a realistic and exciting way. All the characters are extremely well-drawn and Mr Growick, most importantly, does not falter with a very good ear for Holmesian dialogue indeed. Highly recommended. A five-star effort."
The Baker Street Society

www.mxpublishing.com

Also from MX Publishing

The American Literati Series

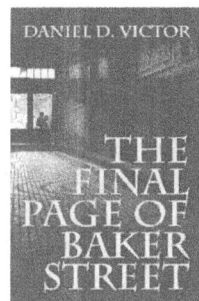  

The Final Page of Baker Street
The Baron of Brede Place
Seventeen Minutes To Baker Street

"The really amazing thing about this book is the author's ability to call up the 'essence' of both the Baker Street 'digs' of Holmes and Watson as well as that of the 'mean streets' of Marlowe's Los Angeles. Although none of the action takes place in either place, Holmes and Watson share a sense of camaraderie and self-confidence in facing threats and problems that also pervades many of the later tales in the Canon. Following their conversations and banter is a return to Edwardian England and its certainties and hope for the future. This is definitely the world before The Great War."
Philip K Jones

www.mxpublishing.com

Also from MX Publishing

The Detective and The Woman Series

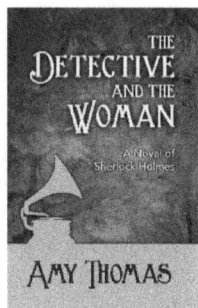  

The Detective and The Woman
The Detective, The Woman and The Winking Tree
The Detective, The Woman and The Silent Hive

"The book is entertaining, puzzling and a lot of fun. I believe the author has hit on the only type of long-term relationship possible for Sherlock Holmes and Irene Adler. The details of the narrative only add force to the romantic defects we expect in both of them and their growth and development are truly marvelous to watch. This is not a love story. Instead, it is a coming-of-age tale starring two of our favorite characters."
Philip K Jones

www.mxpublishing.com

Also from MX Publishing

When the papal apartments are burgled in 1901, Sherlock Holmes is summoned to Rome by Pope Leo XII. After learning from the pontiff that several priceless cameos that could prove compromising to the church, and perhaps determine the future of the newly unified Italy, have been stolen, Holmes is asked to recover them. In a parallel story, Michelangelo, the toast of Rome in 1501 after the unveiling of his Pieta, is commissioned by Pope Alexander VI, the last of the Borgia pontiffs, with creating the cameos that will bedevil Holmes and the papacy four centuries later. For fans of Conan Doyle's immortal detective, the game is always afoot. However, the great detective has never encountered an adversary quite like the one with whom he crosses swords in "The Vatican Cameos.."

"An extravagantly imagined and beautifully written Holmes story"
(**Lee Child**, NY Times Bestselling author, Jack Reacher series)